The Mercenary's Marriage

By Rachel Rossano

Katie,

I hope you enjoy this. Please let me know what you think. ☺

Rachel Rossano

Cover image: *Brice* © 2006 Elizabeth Russell
libbyberrysweet@yahoo.com

For Gregory

Table of Contents

Part I

"There is nothing on this one."

Darius purposely turned his face away from the man who spoke. He hated the necessary collecting of the spoils after every battle. As he rose from his crouch, he scanned the room.

Spotting the king, Darius strode toward him.

"Have they searched every room?" King Simon Jenran of Braulyn asked as Darius approached. The question was directed to the two soldiers who had just arrived.

"No," the older of the two answered wearily, "Just the women's apartments."

"Then keep looking; we must find her," the king instructed. Dismissing the pair with a wave, he turned to face Darius.

"Nothing?" Darius asked as soon as the king's attention was focused on him. As he watched his liege's face, Darius noted the lines deepening around his master's mouth. King Jenran had aged ten years in the past eight months.

The king frowned. "They have not finished looking, but my guess is they will continue to find nothing." He walked to a nearby chair and sank into it. "Has justice been served?" He nodded toward the corpse Darius had been examining.

"Dead," Darius informed him. *And dead too soon,* he added silently. The outcome of this siege was disappointing. Two months spent traveling north and then six months of sitting on their hands. The experience would drag on any warrior. All the time spent in attaining a goal, only to be routed at the last moment with an archer's arrow.

"He died instantly," he added after a pause. The king nodded. Darius did not have to add the rest. They both knew who released the arrow that killed the man: a young man, green with inexperience. It was over and nothing would bring the man back now.

Darius waited as his master thought. The king's bloodshot brown eyes stared off into space. Darius was beginning to think the king had fallen asleep, when he suddenly spoke in a low voice so only Darius could hear. "She was still here this morning." Straightening in his chair, the king continued. "Gwendolyn and her women left a trail only a few hours old." The king met Darius' eyes.

A movement caught the edge of Darius' vision, but he did not acknowledge it. Jenran continued, "If we can determine which direction they took, we might be able to overtake them."

Casually nodding his agreement, Darius swept his gaze across the room. Speaking so only his master could hear, he added, "We have an observer." The man was crouched behind one of the tapestries along the walls. Both exits were two or three hiding places from the hidden man's position.

"Where is he?" The king did not move except to look up and catch Darius's eye as if they were in conversation.

Just then, the figure darted between shelters. Darius felt his mouth drop; he quickly disguised it by saying, "A girl."

"Did you just say it was a girl?" Jenran's weary eyes sharpened and focused more carefully on Darius.

"Yes." Darius carefully turned so he could watch both his master and the girl. "Small build, dark hair, she is definitely not Gwendolyn or one of her frequent companions."

8

The girl darted to the next hiding place. She was one sprint away from freedom. Darius knew how she felt. The tempo of the heart pounding in his chest and the taste of liberty on his tongue were both familiar sensations. "She is mine," he said. He glimpsed the king's smile.

"If you catch her," he agreed.

The girl darted and Darius followed. She disappeared out the door as he silently hurtled the last bench between them.

Brice ran for her life. The empty halls closed in around her and she was certain every sound echoed louder than the last. She needed to get away before someone saw her. Since birth, she heard stories about how mercenaries treated the women captives after a battle. She could not be discovered. Eventually, she found herself in the promenade opening into the inner gardens. The moment her eyes fell on the lush underbrush bordering and overgrowing the paths, she had an idea.

As she turned down the nearest avenue among the trees, Brice caught sight of movement behind her. Was someone following her?

Darius watched the girl run. Automatically stepping with care in his soft leather boots, he had no trouble following the fleeing figure silently. She was quick and a good shadow dancer, but he was better. The training beaten into him since his youth made him superior to almost every man he had ever hunted or faced in battle. Keeping close enough to easily follow her progress, but not close enough to be spotted, Darius studied his choice.

In all the years Darius served Simon Jenran, King of Braulyn, he only asked for two things. He had earned the requests many times over. As a foot soldier, personal guard and now, bodyguard and head of his majesty's personal security force, Darius gave outstanding service and singular dedication. Three years ago, there had been an elaborate plot to take the king's life and then his throne. Darius discovered and foiled the plot at the last minute. In the process, he nearly died.

After he healed from the injuries and returned to service, Jenran promoted him and granted him two requests. For the first, Darius asked for freedom. It was granted immediately. Jenran freed Darius and paid him for all his years of service, making him a very rich man. The second request Darius made was that he would be able to claim something from the spoils of every operation he worked. Jenran granted the request, but Darius never exercised the privilege until today.

Darius was only three feet away the moment the girl spotted the gardens. He slowly closed the gap without allowing himself to be seen. Watching her profile as she turned to look behind her, he knew the moment the idea came to her. She was going to escape. Springing forward as she did, he followed her practically on her heels as she cleared the doorsill and touched down on the moist, moss covered path. He knew her destination, the door on the opposite side of the garden. It was the same one he used only hours before to infiltrate the stronghold. He was not going to let her reach it, however. Looking beyond her bobbing head, he searched for the clearing he knew was coming and waited until the right moment to pounce.

Brice could see the door; it was even standing open. Quickening her speed, she tried to sprint harder. Her muscles protested, but obeyed.

Now she was positive she was being pursued; she just did not know how closely. For one crazy second, she believed if she could just make it through the door, she would be free and safe. But the feeling lasted only for that moment, for in the next, her foot landed wrong.

Something hard, heavy, and huge struck her from behind. The ground rose up to meet her at a dangerous rate. She tried to put out her hands and catch herself, but they were pinned to her sides. All she could do was close her eyes and brace herself for the impact. Something large, warm, and living wrapped itself around her at the last moment. With a deft twist in mid air and a hard jolt, Brice came to an abrupt, but surprisingly gentle, stop.

Fearing who might have caught her, Brice pushed against whatever it was confining her only to find it unrelenting.

"Don't I at least get a thank you?" A deep voice asked from behind her left ear. "It is the least a rescuer should receive for saving a lady's pretty neck."

"I am not a lady." Brice pushed again against the stranger's arms. This time they released her, reluctantly. Quickly scrambling for her feet, she stepped away from the man only to find him already on his own feet and watching her warily. Inwardly grimacing, Brice noticed the small gate behind the strange man's right shoulder.

"It is safer in here." The man's voice brought her eyes and thoughts back to him. He was huge and dark. Brice struggled not to shiver or give in to the cold tingle at the base of her spine.

"I doubt it," she finally managed while she tried to judge how much of a head start she was going to need to make it to freedom and close the gate behind her. The sturdy wooden door with its iron hinges would hold him for a few minutes. Time enough for her to get away.

"I would remove the hinges." This time his voice was tinged with a hint of an accent. Brice brought her eyes back to his face and was annoyed to find a pair of dark gray eyes laughing at her. This was all a game for him she realized. A game he was confident he would win. "There are also men out there looking for your mistress, Lady Gwendolyn. They would not be as patient with you as I am being."

Brice studied him for a moment. He was very tall, over six feet. In her experience, tall men usually depended on their size to compensate for speed and agility, but this man obviously had both. From the way he was balancing on the

11

front part of his feet, he believed she was going to run. When she raised her eyes to study his face, she found those strange gray eyes studying her in return.

"Do you like what you see?" His accent was gone, but his eyes were still smiling in spite of an impassive face.

Choosing not to answer the question, Brice asked, "What do you want with me?"

His eyes suddenly sobered. "It depends."

After a few moments of uneasy silence, Brice finally asked, "On what?"

"Whether or not you cooperate," he replied. Sounds started coming from the direction of the castle. The man did not break his eye contact with her.

"And if I don't?" Brice asked. The noise became the sound of many armored feet striking stone at a measured trot.

"I will have to take you by force and convince the men that you belong to me." He frowned. "I do not think you would enjoy it."

The coming group was going to spot them standing in the center of the garden at any moment. "And the alternative…" Brice readied to make a dash for it. She would go down fighting if necessary.

"You trust me to protect you now and explain later." He slowly offered her his hand, extending it palm up between them. "Come silently and I promise not to hurt you."

Brice heard the cries as one of the men spotted them. She was running out of time, and he knew it. Still she could not decide. *If he had wanted to hurt me, he would have made a move before now.* Dropping her eyes to the man's hand, Brice desperately thought. *Who do I fear more? This man is at least giving me a choice. The men coming will not.* With the decision made, she stepped forward and reached toward his fingers.

Darius did not wait for their hands to touch. He did not have time. Mentally wincing at the fear he saw written across the girl's face the moment before he caught her up, he jumped into action. In order for him to pull off not having to demonstrate his possession of the only female plunder, they must disappear immediately. Catching the girl around the waist, Darius dove for the nearest cover, an ancient pine with ground sweeping branches. By ducking beneath their curtain and putting the trunk between the two of them and their previous position, they disappeared from view. Positioning the girl against the opposite side of the trunk, he effectively blocked anyone from seeing her if they did not look closely.

Wisely, the female did not scream. Darius looked down at her the moment they were hidden. She was grabbing the trunk behind her as if it was the only anchor in the world. She leaned her head back against the bark, giving Darius a full view of tightly closed eyes framed by a mass of dark brown curls falling free of their binding. The harsh angles of her face hinted that she had been without adequate food for a while. As he had ascertained before, she was smaller than most women, but she obviously had the spirit to make up for her size.

"Where did he go?" Voices rose as the men came to an abrupt stop where they two of them had been standing moments before.

"What are you men doing out there?" A voice called out from the parapets over looking the enclosed garden. Immediately every man in the group tensed and their apparent leader saluted to someone out of Darius' sight.

"We thought we saw someone out here, sir." The leader below called.

"The gardens have already been searched," the unseen man informed them. "Take your detail into the dungeons. They have not been investigated yet. Keep your eyes open for secret passages or hidden rooms."

Obediently, the group reformed their ranks and trot-marched in the direction of the nearest entrance. Darius watched and listened until all the echoes dwindled away to nothing. The small girl he was trapping against the tree

13

stopped trembling. Looking down to make sure she had not
chosen the escape of the pampered lady and fainted on him, he
encountered her grave green eyes examining his face.

He did not look cruel. Brice came to this conclusion in
spite of the minor scars marring the smoothness of his face.
Maybe it was because his eyes were so expressive. She was
wondering how the largest and deepest of his scars affected
his smile. It started near his temple and made an almost
smooth path to about an inch above his jaw line. It was old
and had long healed to the darkness of damaged skin. Then he
turned from his scrutiny of the building and looked at her. All
thoughts of his face immediately vanished from her mind.

"We are going back in." He must have seen the
surprise and fear that crossed her mind for he continued.
"Stay with me and you will be safe. The men will not bother
you now I have claimed you as mine."

"Will you have to…" she had forgotten the words he
had used. She looked away. It was hard to think with those
eyes watching.

"Convince them," he said for her. She looked up to
find his eyes laughing again. The laughter did not reach his
the rest of his face though.

"Will you?" She asked.

"For your sake, let us hope not." He stepped away and
offered her his hand. "Come, now is our best chance."
Hesitant, but uncertain she had any alternative; Brice took it.
Immediately his large warm hand gripped hers and he headed
to the entrance opposite the way from the men had taken.

She was small and her legs so much shorter than his;
Darius found himself adjusting his stride so he was not
dragging her along behind him. He needed to get back to the
king. The girl might know something useful.

She stopped and dug in her heels the moment the
entrance to the hall was in sight. He delayed his reaction until

he had pulled her behind the heavy column next to the door. Turning, he backed her up by her shoulders into the shadow of the wooden pillar and blocked the only escape. He towered over her in a way that anyone who saw him would not be able to see her, though they would definitely wonder what he was doing facing a wall.

"I need to report to the King," he told her. She was shaking so badly he could hear her teeth chattering. Most likely, the memories of the massacre that had taken place in the room were now filling her mind. He had not removed his hands yet and he was afraid if he did now, she would collapse. "He is going to have a few questions for you, but after that, I might be leaving you with him." Moving his hands from her shoulders to each side of her head, he lifted her face so she was forced to meet his eyes. Their green depths were glinting with unshed tears and her bottom lip trembled despite her obvious fiery resolve that it not. "If you wish to be safe, stay with the King if I leave. He will enforce my claim on you, but if you leave his presence, I cannot vouch for what will happen. Do you understand?"

She nodded slightly before pulling her head from his hands to again study the hard tile floor.

"Ay, Darius." A voice called from behind Darius. Darius turned away from the girl to greet Ewian. "I have been looking for you all over. What did you find in the garden that the others were so...." The man stopped abruptly when he caught sight of the girl. "Ah, a little brown bird." He smiled slowly. "I would not wish to share her either." Darius did not allow his annoyance to show; countryman or not, Ewian had better keep his distance from this little brown bird.

"I was about to report to King Jenran," Darius said. "Are you doing the same?"

"Oh, no." Ewian took a step in the opposite direction. "I was just looking for you. I will be going now." He quickly disappeared the way he had come.

"The King will only want to ask some questions," the

15

man said again when the other had disappeared. The other man had looked similar in coloring to her captor, but his eyes had been brown and his build not as tall. Bracing his arm against the column to her left, the one called Darius leaned down closer to her face. "Remember you are not out of danger yet." Brice found her eyes looking into his. "The king will honor my claim. Near him or me you will be safe; but anywhere else until the word has spread you are in grave danger. See you do not leave my side."

Abruptly he drew back and took her hand again. Turning, he thrust open the door and strode back into the room she had fled only moments before. Brice willed herself not to panic as she was pulled with him.

She swallowed carefully and looked around. The room was much the same as she had last seen it. There were fewer men moving about and her master's body was covered with the hearthrug, but the tables were still overturned and the red-haired man still sat in the master's carved chair. Her captor made his way directly to this man. Pausing in his approach, a few feet from the man, he bowed and shot her a glare. Getting the idea she was supposed to show respect, Brice managed a weak curtsy. She would have fallen over if he had released her hand.

"Ah, Darius, a successful pursuit, I see," the red haired man said. "Rise and approach; I wish to question the girl." Lifting her head, Brice found the new man's eyes on her face. They were dark brown. After a gentle prod from her companion, Brice stepped closer as the man looked her over.

"What is your name?" He was looking with interest at her bare feet. She felt her ears warm. They were probably muddy after the trip through the garden.

"Brice, sir," she answered.

"Sire or your majesty," her captor informed her.

Brice's eyes flew to the red-haired man's head; only then did she see the gold circlet among the dark curls. She immediately dropped her eyes and wished the ground would swallow her. "Pardon me." She had no doubt her ears were

16

red. Thankful they were beneath her hair, she corrected herself, "Your Majesty."

"'Sire' is fine, child." The king actually smiled. He then addressed the man behind her. "Where did you catch her?"

"The garden, Sire," the man answered. "She was making for the back gate."

The king nodded and then asked, "Slave or free?"

"Slave," the man said. Brice almost touched the heavy leather collar around her neck, but managed the last minute to restrain herself. It was well hidden beneath her clothing.

"Whose?" The king returned to looking her over.

"I would guess she was a lady's maid from her hands. The calluses are not hard enough for a kitchen wench." Brice felt the man shift. "But she runs like one accustomed to running." The mercenary's thoughtful tone sent shivers up her back. *What else did he know?*

"What do you mean, Darius?" The king asked. Brice felt his eyes leave their survey of her and meet the man's over her head.

"She was not always a lady's maid."

"Well, then, lady's maid," the king said engaging Brice's eyes. "Were you in contact with the lord's daughter, Gwendolyn?"

"Yes, sire."

"Was she well?"

"Yes, sire." That was an odd question to ask her.

"And the babe?"

This time there was no mistaking the oddness. Brice was confused. "What babe, sire?"

"Has not Gwendolyn recently given birth to a child?" The king's face was at total odds with his tone. His voice was inquisitive, but his eyes were calm, cold, and calculating. "Or perhaps she has suffered a miscarriage within the past few months?"

"Is she large with child?" the man behind her asked.

"None of these things are true," Brice found herself saying. Had these men gone mad?

Surprise crossed the king's face as he dropped his eyes. After a moment, he rose from his chair in one smooth movement and crossed to the covered body only a few feet away. "Micrey," the king said to the corpse, "You were too crafty for your own good."

"There was no child." The voice behind her was weary sounding. Brice turned to look at the man the King called Darius. When he met her eyes, she was surprised to find them to be sorrowful.

Just then, the main doors opened with a crash and the other Ratharian and a large group of men entered dragging a young farmer.

"Sire, we found this man hiding in the wine cellar."

The king nodded and waved them away. "Have my horse brought up to the entrance. We are returning to camp."

The men retreated and the Ratharian paused long enough to bow and say, "Yes sire," before disappearing after them.

"We break camp tonight." The red-haired ruler abruptly declared. "Darius, see that the orders are spread." Turning to leave, the king would have left the room, except Darius, her captor, spoke.

"I wish to have my claim be made legal."

The king paused and turned to regard Darius. "Why? The other men…" he broke off. "Very well," he said as he turned back toward the door. "When we reach camp, I will see what I can manage." He disappeared through the open door.

"Come." Darius directed the order toward the girl. She turned a puzzled face toward him.

"Why did you attack us?"

Darius blinked. It took him a moment to realize that

she wanted to know the purpose of the siege and the attack. Obviously, she would be aware of the drama playing out around her and would have questions.

"Later." He started toward the door the king had just used. Turning back to see if she was following, he found she had not moved. He clarified, "I will answer your questions later; I promise."

For a moment, Darius wondered if he was going to need to use force again to bring her along. Wishing with all his heart there was more time to reassure her, he took a step back in her direction. "I will come," she said. He looked up to see her eyes watching him with a mixture of fear and confusion.

"Then, come," he replied. He crossed to the door and swung it open as she approached. Obediently, she followed.

Darius put his arm protectively around her shoulders the moment they stepped into the hall. He drew her along with him as he made his way to the main courtyard, where the king would be preparing to ride out to their camp outside the curtain walls.

Part II

Brice initially was uncomfortable with the mercenary's arm across her shoulders. He was very tall and the closeness of his frame made her feel even more insignificant and weak. He seemed to be making his way to the main courtyard, which was probably where the king was preparing to leave. After assessing that fact, Brice concentrated on keeping up with the man's long strides.

"Have you ever ridden?" Darius asked suddenly.

Shaking her head, Brice managed a breathless, "No."

"Then you best ride with me," he announced as they approached the main doors. Pausing before they reached them, he turned her to face him and glanced quickly up and down her body. "No shoes, no cloak," he muttered. "Guess we will have to make do." He smiled down at her and Brice felt her mouth drop open. His smile was amazing when it involved his whole face.

Ignoring her reaction, Darius swept the door open and stepped out into the courtyard. The air had cooled considerably and an instant chill traveled up Brice's legs from the cold cobbles beneath her feet. The space was loud with the chaos of a departing troop. Horses neighing, men shouting, and the sound of metal horseshoes on stone echoed against the barren walls. The raw volume made Brice want to cover her ears, but she found she could not. His grip on her forearm was too strong.

The mercenary pulled her with him into the wild madness and she soon found herself praying he would not lose her. He was the only stable island amid the sea of horses' legs, rushing men, and dogs. *Where did the dogs come from?* She hadn't noticed any signs of dogs before. Suddenly she was thankful her captor had prevented her from running. She witnessed enough hunts in her lifetime to know how an animal was brought down by a pack of hounds. The insane fear of the hunted creature was frightening to see let alone experience.

"There you are." A voice broke through the loud clamor from above them. Looking up, Brice could just make out the outline of a man on horseback. "Your horse is over by the stables." The horse stepped sideways with a plaintive whinny as a man next to his head hollered a curse at the top of his lungs. A massive hoof came down heavy, only inches from Brice's foot. Instantly she shrunk back against the very solid form of the man behind her. Without looking from the horseman's face, Darius enfolded her within the fall of his cloak and almost completely behind his body.

"Meet you back at camp," the stranger called as he urged his beast into the churning mass, and then he was gone.

"Which way are the stables from here?" her protector asked without looking down. "We need to leave before the looters are all that are left."

"To the left of the main entrance," Brice offered. She had no idea where they were now, so she could not offer more detailed directions. Thankfully, the mercenary did not seem to need them. He nodded and started to move through the madness.

In a matter of moments, Brice found herself standing by the flank of a caramel colored stallion. Darius made quick work of the knotted reins. Throwing them over the horse's head, he turned back to her. Without a word, he wrapped his hands around her ribs and hoisted her onto the horse's back. Before Brice could even begin looking for something to

21

balance herself with, he was behind her. Clamping a hard arm around her midriff, he took the reins, and with a shout, the horse beneath them lunged toward the gate.

Closing her eyes against the rise of her stomach, Brice was sure she was going to be bounced apart. The arm around her waist tightened. "Relax," he demanded. "The ride will be much easier if you relax and move with the horse." With all her concentration, Brice tried to obey, but there was little change. Just as she thought she was getting the hang of the rhythm, the beast slowed. She opened her eyes to the sight of passing tents and hurrying men. The horse slowed even more as they approached a larger tent in the center of the mass. The Ratharian from the castle was just exiting when the mercenary brought them up to the front.

"Ewian." Her captor swung down and reached up for her without looking to see if the man had stopped. "I need you to take care of the horse." Lifting her effortlessly, he placed her on the ground and made sure she was steady on her feet before turning to other soldier. "Is the king ready for me?"

Ewian nodded, "Yes, but you must hurry. His aides are already packing up and will get to the documents soon." The man caught the horse's bobbing harness and began leading him away.

"Come," Darius said as he turned toward the canvas structure. "You will be safer if I have legal claim."

Still confused as to what the man meant Brice obediently followed him into the dark interior.

The girl was tense and in spite of her obvious exhaustion, agitated. Fear was evident in her every motion and Darius did not blame her. In her position, he would have been spitting mad and demanding answers. But as much as he felt for her, he had to go through with this to protect her and her future.

The king was indeed waiting for them. His scribe, an older man, was the only other in the small foyer of the tent.

Although visually they were alone, scuffling and voices from behind the curtained doorways into other parts of the structure reminded Darius they were not.

"There you are." The king greeted them as soon as they entered. "Come closer." He waved at them to move deeper into the room. "Keiter needs your full names for the records. Darius, you go first." Walking toward his portable council seat, the king left them to the scribe.

"Darius Aarin Laris," he told the man, who quickly scratched the letters onto his parchment. Darius did not bother spelling it. His witness was needed on enough documents and treaties that Keiter knew the letters. Turning to the girl, Darius nodded toward the scribe.

"Brice Wrlyn Ashlyn." She formed the sounds as if they were a treasure reluctantly relinquished. "What is this for?" Her voice wavered, but the question was clear.

"Darius wishes to make legal claim as your protector and provider," the king answered from his seat beyond them. "He wishes to marry you, child." Darius stepped back to give her clear view of the king, but kept his eyes on her face. He needed to know how she reacted to this revelation.

She stepped toward the king. Darius could no longer see her face. "Why, sire?"

The king smiled at her. "You are going to have to ask him that."

Darius waited in silence. For some strange reason, his chest ached and his throat was tight. Instead of turning to face him, the girl answered her own question, "To protect me. To have legal claim." Her voice was thoughtful but uncertain.

"Let me give you some insight." The king leaned forward. "Darius always has a reason, but rarely does he share it. From experience, I have learned to accept that and trust him." The candid praise settled uneasily on Darius, but the girl turned to look back at him with a measuring shadow in her green eyes. Then the king asked the essential question. "Are you willing to bind yourself to this man?" Darius held his breath.

23

Brice's eyes lowered and Darius' heart sank. Instantly his mind began working out alternatives. He had to keep her near and safe; that was certain. If he established her with the servants at the castle when they returned, she would be relatively safe, but he would rarely see her. A position as a lady's maid was even more isolated from his world within the castle.

"Yes," Brice answered.

Darius' eyes focused once again on her doubt-filled face.

"Then let us get this finished so we can all go home," The king declared, pushing himself wearily to his feet. "Approach me." The scribe produced a small package and handed it to the king as they obeyed. "Join hands," he instructed as he turned to face them.

Darius offered his right hand, palm up, to Brice. She looked at it uncertainly and then shot a brief glance at his face before timidly placing her right hand there. Slowly and gently, Darius enfolded her small fingers in his much larger hand. *I promise to take care of it,* he thought. Brice did not raise her eyes from the joining. She just stood there silent and motionless as the king began to intone the words that would bind them forever.

He is so much larger than you. He is a complete stranger. Why do you trust him? Why are you doing this? Weakly, Brice answered her inner voice. *Because I have no other choice.* Then, she desperately attempted to concentrate on anything other than the tall, dark man standing beside her. She also desperately tried to ignore the tender way he was holding her hand. She was concentrating so hard that when the king started to wrap a long piece of silk around their joined hands, she startled. The soldier's hand tightened around hers and the king stopped mid word. Even if she wanted to withdraw her hand, the man's grasp would have prevented her. Somehow, though, Brice knew if she asked, he would let go.

An uneasy silence hung between them for a moment.

24

All she could hear was the servants' movement on the other side of the curtains.

Finally, the king continued. "Bound together until time is no more, bound to each as to none before." The silk wrapped around for the second time. "Bound before man, sovereign, and God." A third strip fell into place, completely covering their clasped hands. Taking the ends, which now dangled unevenly, the king knotted them over the point of union. "With a binding that will never break." He pulled the knot snug. "You are man and wife before God, king, and man. May it be a blessing and never a curse."

With great effort, Brice raised her face to her husband. She found him silently watching her with a look in his dark gray eyes that she could not yet interpret.

They left the king's tent and Darius immediately noticed the sag of his new wife's shoulders. Then remembering her bare feet, he leaned over and lifted her into his arms. He half expected her to fight or at least vocally protest, but she did neither. Her head fell to his shoulder and the small body in his arms relaxed against him. "Thank you." She sighed and he guessed she fell almost instantly asleep.

When he arrived at his own tent, he found his armor bearer busily packing. The boy's name was Timothy and he was an energetic young man with a quiet disposition much like Darius'. The two of them were companions of many years now and comfortable with each other's habits. As expected, Timothy was not anticipating this.

"Who is that?" He finally managed as he stared at the motionless form in Darius' arms. Darius watched as the boy took in the bare feet sticking out over his arm. "Where are the shoes?"

"I don't know." Darius jutted his chin toward the larger of the two cots. "Clear off the cot. After I set her down, I will explain."

Clearing the cot took only a moment. Timothy watched with wide eyes as Darius gently lowered Brice onto it. "So it is a girl?" The boy asked.

"Yes." Darius took off his cloak. With his usual efficiency, Timothy had already packed the blankets. Spreading his cloak like a covering, he said, "She is my wife."

Timothy dropped the armor-cleaning satchel he removed from the cot. Darius winced at the clatter it made hitting the ground and looked over at the girl. All she did was turn her head to face the tent wall, and then, with a sigh, her breathing settled back into the slow cadence of sleep.

As soon as he was sure she was not going to wake, Darius turned to his shocked assistant. "Show some care," he hissed, waving at the heap at the boy's feet. "She has had a long and traumatizing day."

"I am sure marrying you had nothing to do with it." The boy shot back in a low tone. "Where did you find her? Why did you marry her? What is wrong with your head?" The willowy boy gestured emphatically.

Holding up a hand to slow the flow of questions being hurled at him, Darius put his finger to his lips and gestured toward the door. The boy obeyed with a frown. Darius followed.

Camp was settling down a bit as most of the men completed their packing and were trying to catch a few hours of sleep before the dawn move out. Darius and Timothy faced each other across the entrance to their tent and conversed in whispers.

"I found her in the castle," Darius began. "She was a servant to the lord's daughter."

"Gwendolyn's maid, ay," Timothy interrupted. "She knows something you or the king needs?"

Shaking his head, Darius said, "She already told us all we needed to know. Gwendolyn was never with child." Timothy's eyes got large as the implications of the statement dawned on him.

"You mean we have just wasted eight months chasing a shadow plot?"

"The king has ordered the army home," Darius reminded the boy. "I only hope there is no surprise for us when we get there."

"Do you mean Micrey was only a decoy?" Timothy asked.

"Or the mastermind of a larger plot."

"So, that is why he visited all those other Lords before arriving at his fortress here," the boy said. "He was trying to raise support. But support for what?"

"That is what I am concerned about," Darius said as he took a seat beside the fire pit. "I only hope Micrey didn't get a warm reception with his fellow lords. If he did, we might have more than we can deal with when we return to Kiylin. The Queen was in no condition to subdue a rebellion when we left."

The boy nodded his agreement. They fell into silence for a while and then Timothy asked pointedly, "So why did you pick her? And why marry her? You could have enjoyed giving her a tumble without the responsibility afterwards."

Righteous indignation rose in a storm. Before he quite knew what he was doing, Darius had risen and struck the boy full across the mouth. "I cannot believe you said that. You have been hanging around the other boys too much." Timothy watched him warily and Darius did not blame him. He had never punished the boy with his hand before and he felt awful, but he could not back down. The boy needed to know that Brice was now part of their group and a part to be respected. "I never want to hear it again, especially not in her presence. Do you understand?"

Mutely the boy nodded. Then he asked, "So why did you marry her?"

After a moment, Darius admitted something he had been avoiding since he had first set eyes on her crouched figure behind the tapestry. "Instinct," he sighed tiredly. "Now I am going to try to get a few hours rest. I suggest you finish as silently as you can while I sleep. Wake me at the first horn blast." The boy nodded. "Thanks, Timothy." He threw the youngster an affectionate smile before reentering the tent.

A loud blast on what sounded like a battle horn brought Brice's eyes wide open. She probably would have jumped from the bed too, but a heavy arm was wrapped around her waist. As her other senses awoke, she noticed the heavy blanket over her and a warm body heating her from behind. Blinking to clear her eyes, she slowly focused them on the dirty canvas wall only inches from her face.

"Darius," a young man's voice called and someone jostled the cot. "Time to move." The warmth at her back moved with a groan and then lifted away. Shivering against the sudden draft, Brice carefully rolled over. She encountered a wide, cloth covered back.

"I'm up, Timothy," the man on the edge of the bed growled. "Go fetch the horses." A brief flash of early morning light blinded Brice for a moment as Timothy left the tent to obey. When her vision cleared, she found a pair of gray eyes watching her from above. "I hope you are a little refreshed from last night." The voice was laced with a hint of accent again and the eyes were softer than before.

"A little," she managed as she tried not to blush.

"We have a long day of travel ahead," he said and pushed off the cot and to his feet.

"Where are we going?" Brice asked as she carefully followed him off the cot. She hated the feeling of him towering over her. She turned back to fold the cover only to find it was his dark brown cloak from the night before.

"To Kiylin, the king's main residence," he answered. Brice had heard of the fortress. She turned to find him pulling on his boots. His eyes were on her feet. "Later today I will ask the supply master to see if we can find you some boots." Rising, he crossed to pick up a long cloak from the other chair. "It appears Timothy has already found a temporary cloak for you." The gray fabric looked worn, but still useful. Darius crossed to her. Removing the dark brown one from her hands, he draped the gray around her shoulders. "It looks like an old

28

one of mine."

Finding herself swamped by gray fabric, Brice felt a bit overwhelmed. Long fingers firmly fastened the clasp and raised the hood to almost hide her face from sight. "There," the warrior before her declared, "You can hide from everything in there." Lifting the edge of the hood and peeking from beneath it, Brice was surprised at the laughter in the man's eyes. It promptly disappeared though. Another loud blast vibrated though the camp. "Come," he instructed and strode to the entrance of the tent. Gathering the excess material like a highborn lady gathers her skirt, Brice hurried to obey.

The morning passed smoothly once Brice grew accustomed to the horse's lolling gait. The company traveled at the speed of the foot soldiers and Darius stayed near the king. Before mounting, he had donned many pieces of gear including a large sword. Brice initially found sharing the saddle with a fully armed mercenary awkward, but eventually she became comfortable with his constant arm around her waist and strong presence at her back.

In the late morning, the company stopped for a quick meal. Before they ate, Darius decided to bring her to see the supply master. Weaving back through the large wagons that had lumbered along behind them, Darius brought her directly up to the largest one. "Master Kline, I have a challenge for you," he said to the elderly man sitting in the shade of the wagon.

"So you say, my boy," the man answered before looking up from his harness mending. "I have been outfitting soldiers, archers, and all manner of warriors for many years. What kind of challenge could you offer me?"

"A rare one I am sure." Darius waved Brice forward. "This woman needs clothing and foot gear."

The man's eyes widened and carefully looked her up and down. "Take off the cloak, child," he instructed, "And help me up, boy." Flapping a hand at Darius, he readied himself to rise. Dutifully, Darius took the older man's flailing limb and pulled him to his feet. The man immediately began to circle Brice and mutter to himself. Darius took her cloak and stepped back. Folding his arms across his chest, he stood there, watchfully waiting.

"So where did he find you?" Master Kline asked before tugging at Brice's dirt-covered skirt. Only the morning before it had been one of her best, but after the tumble in the dirt, a night's sleep, and so much time on the horse, the material was never going to be the same.

"Well, child," the older man prompted her as he frowned on her dirty bare feet. "Don't tell me he found you in a palace." He winked at her and then went back to frowning. "Obviously he does not know how to treat a lady." Clicking his tongue and wagging his head, he turned to Darius. "You have much to learn, boy."

"Just dress her, Kline, and stop lecturing me." Darius did not sound pleased with the Master Kline. The older man, however, did not seem bothered by the prospect of a large foreign mercenary being angry with him.

"The cloak just needs hemming, which you can do yourself, right child?" He raised a questioning eyebrow.

Brice nodded.

"Good." Standing back, the man began to stroke his scruffy chin. "All the boots I have will be too big, but how do some leather shoes sound?" Master Kline looked over at the soldier.

Darius nodded. "She will be spending most of her time on my horse, not her feet. That should suit."

"I have a rather worn tunic and surcoat somewhere that will hold up better than this flimsy stuff." The man lifted some of Brice's skirt. The dress had never been fancy, but it was not made for travel either.

"How soon?" Darius asked.

"This evening," Kline answered. "I will also provide a needle, thread and scissors for her cloak. Now move on, you two, I have work to do." Turning, he headed back toward his wagon.

"Come." Darius took her cloak and wrapped it around her shoulders. "I am sure you are hungry."

After making sure the clasp was secure, Darius led her back toward their earlier position. His large straight back was easy to follow, but she found it difficult to keep up with his stride. His legs were so much longer than hers. As they passed other companies gathered around the meal wagons, Brice's mouth began to water. Yes, she was hungry.

They stopped in the late afternoon near a river, but neither one of them dismounted. Brice longed to stretch her numb legs and aching back, but Darius had other ideas. He guided their mount straight into the river. Brice tensed as the animal's head lowered to drink. The muscles in her back clenched and she carefully peered down past her feet. Swift-flowing water coursed between the horse's legs. The animal was standing knee high in the river.

"We are just stopping for the horses to drink," Darius said from behind her. The horse slurped loudly to emphasize the obvious. A heavy silence fell between them. Brice looked around. Other horses were similarly occupied, but none were as far from shore as them.

Darius sighed. "I was going to wait until tonight to do this, but since we must wait for the horses…." He shifted his weight and used the arm that had been around her waist to reach for something. Brice panicked. Curling her fingers around the front edge of the saddle, she prayed desperately the beast would not move. All it would take was a small nudge and she would fall right into the river. "There it is," her companion muttered. "Hold still."

Rough leather covered fingers encircled the left side of her neck. Brice shivered and forgot about her fear of falling. *What is he doing?* Her throat closed and she considered screaming. *Who would stop him?* No one would. He could do as he willed with her. She was his property. A glint in her

31

peripheral vision was the only warning she was given before cold metal touched her throat.

"Hold still," Darius instructed again. Tears filled Brice's eyes. *He is going to kill me,* she thought as the metal moved against her skin. She squeezed her eyes closed and willed the tears not to fall. *I will not die a coward. Courage.* Her heart raced as his grip on her slave collar tightened. Then suddenly, with a sharp jerk, it was gone; her collar was gone.

No sooner had she realized what he had just done than his hand was back at her throat. Tilting her chin up, he bent his head to examine her neck.

"Good," he said mildly. He sheathed his blade and then asked, "Do you want to keep it?" He extended his left hand so she could see the strip of leather that lay there. It was strange looking, lying there limp and broken. Brice never thought she would see it in someone's hand. Shaking, she turned her face away. "I don't blame you," he said. Flinging it into the water, Darius gathered the reins and urged the horse to raise his head.

Tears coursed down Brice's face. They were not tears of joy. *I don't understand.* She had never felt so confused and afraid in her life. *This man does not make sense and it scares me.*

"We will reach Kiylin in a few days," Darius told Brice later that afternoon. The horse beneath them whinnied and shook his head. Brice did not respond. "Timothy and I live in a house in the servants' village." The girl shifted sleepily. She had not had much rest last night and he had no idea how well she had been able to sleep the nights before the siege broke. Sliding the arm around her waist higher, he tried to encourage her to lean against him. She resisted. He loosened his grip. "It is not much, but Timothy and I are comfortable there."

"Why don't you live in the castle?" She asked.

"The servants of the castle know more about what is really going on than the inhabitants." He explained. "I also like to get away from the intrigue and politics when I am off duty."

"How often is that?"

He smiled. She was interested. "I am on scheduled duty almost daily for four or more hours at a time. The king's needs vary and he sends for me when he needs me. I travel when the king travels, unless he wishes for me to be protecting someone or something else."

"Like the queen?"

He nodded. "Like the queen, or one of the princes."

They rode in silence for a while. Brice's head kept dropping forward and the curls escaping her braid would fall into her face. Jerking herself awake, she would suddenly straighten and push them out of her face again. After a particularly sudden movement from Brice, their horse snorted a complaint and sped up briefly.

"You really should lean back against me, Brice," Darius pointed out. "Next time, he might bolt. I promise I will not let you slip."

At first, Brice continued to sit poker straight and face forward as though she had not heard him. Then, slowly her shoulders lowered and reluctantly she responded, "Very well."

Allowing his arm to pull her closer, she leaned back against him. Bringing his shoulders forward and tightening his grip, Darius fitted her smaller frame against his. Drawing his cloak about them, he almost hid her from view. "Sleep easy," he murmured, although he suspected from the relaxed way she sank against him, she was already almost asleep.

What have I gotten myself into? He wondered as he caught the King's amused glance their way.

"We can send out messengers," Arcan, King Jenran's chief advisor, announced his solution to the group. They were gathered in King Jenran's tent after a long day of travel. Darius stood at attention at his post to Jenran's left. To the king's right stood Darius' friend, Ewian. Gathered around them were the highest-ranking men in their army. General Trinight frowned at Arcan.

"Even if we sent men yesterday, the Lords would not have sufficient time to send help for our arrival at Kiylin." The General gestured toward Trenar, the chief of the King's intelligence and declared, "I vote we use those men to scout out ahead. I would like to know what we are walking into. That way we can strategize our assault, if necessary. It will increase our chances of success. If Kiylin is indeed under rebel control, we will need the best strategy we can develop."

"First, we need to know how widespread this rebellion is." Lord Tiren pointed out as he rose to his feet. "We do not know if Micrey received support or rejection from those stops he made on his way from Kiylin to his vargar. If he received support, Kiylin is the least of our worries, for we will have to find an ally and gather forces for defense of the King. If Micrey received a cool reception, we can focus our efforts on Kiylin and plan accordingly."

"So," Arcan said as he looked over at the General. "We are back to sending messengers."

"No." Trenar's voice cut across Arcan's with a tone of authority. "We know that Micrey received very cold greetings from all but one of the lords he sought." Then, he fell silent.

"And…" Arcan prompted.

"The king has already been informed and the traitor will be dealt with." Trenar glanced at the King and received a nod in return. The room fell silent. "As to the current situation, I would advise that we send a scout ahead to Kiylin to assess what awaits us there. Meanwhile, the army should follow at the fastest pace possible. My quickest man should be able to make the trip there and back in three days."

"Then that is what we will do." The King announced his decision before any could comment more. "You may leave me," he said standing to his feet. Then he turned to Darius and Ewian. "You both come with me."

Darius and Ewian followed him through the flap into his sleeping area. A meal lay on a low table and the king seated himself at the end. Motioning for them to stand before him, he leaned forward with a frown. "I am not content with waiting. The Queen was not in the best of health when we left Kiylin and I am eager to hear news of her. As you both know, I have sent messages to her repeatedly since we cornered Micrey. None of them were answered and the messengers did not return. Trenar believes that they were intercepted and I am losing patience. If we do not have news by the end to two days, I am taking a group of men and traveling ahead."

"Sire," Ewian said. "I fear that would be foolhardy. The decreased numbers would put you at risk."

"Not if there are traitors in our midst even now, as Trenar believes. His men have seen signs that someone is stealing our supplies and sending information to an unknown contact. One message was intercepted that hinted at my death. He is still trying to corner the leak, but it is difficult in an army two thousand strong." He sighed. "I may be safer among a group of handpicked men, loyal only to me. Even if they are fewer in number, I will not have to be concerned about finding an assassin's knife in my back. I have not decided on the matter, but I want you both to be ready to leave at a moment's notice."

Darius nodded, but his heart was heavy with indecision. "Sire, if there is danger, you should have someone guarding you more closely."

The King smiled. "Trenar and Regan have already tightened my security far more than I can stand. I sleep with my sword at my side as I did when I was fighting for the throne in my youth. Go and be at peace, Darius. I am as safe as I can be at this moment. I just do not wish to go into the battle for Kiylin defending my back as well as my front."

"Very well, Sire."

"I had to argue with the mess master for twenty minutes just to get this." Timothy, Darius' armor bearer's voice carried clearly in the night air. Brice heard it perfectly through the tent wall and the heavy wool fabric of the dress she was attempting to pull over her head. She did not hear Darius' reply, but Timothy's reaction was very understandable.

"Fine," he said in a sulky tone. "I will try again. Maybe this time he will believe there are three in our tent." As he stomped off, Brice finished smoothly rolling her old dress into a ball. Then taking up the gray cloak and the small bag of sewing supplies the supply master sent over, she went to find some light.

Outside the tent flap, a good fire was burning a few yards away. A dark crouching shadow, Brice assumed was Darius, loomed next to it. She picked her way carefully to his side and sat down. Then she dumped the contents of the sewing kit into her lap.

She was just about to cut the excess off the cape bottom, when Darius spoke. "I promised to explain why we came."

Brice looked up, but Darius was staring into the fire before them and did not return her glance.

"The king has four sons." His voice was deep and there was no trace of accent as he turned his eyes to the stick in his hands. Rolling it between his palms, he continued, "The eldest, Tyrone, is like his father. The second, a rash and bold troublemaker, is named Maler. He is the favorite because he is like the king was when he was young. The last two are younglings, not old enough to cause much trouble. They are too busy learning to be great lords to be personally active in any political plots."

Discarding the stick into the fire, Darius leaned forward and rested his forearms on his knees. "Lord Micrey wanted an alliance between his house and the royal house. When he offered an arrangement between his daughter, Gwendolyn, and one of the king's sons, the king turned him down. Not at all deterred, he arranged for Gwendolyn to be caught unchaperoned in the embrace of Tyrone, the heir. When he grasped, Lord Micrey reached for the best.

"As soon as the rumors of an affair were well underway, he took his daughter and left the city in the dead of night without warning. The moment they were gone, a slave appeared at the palace gate, demanding he had a message for the king. Micrey claimed his daughter was compromised and with child by Tyrone."

Darius shifted again, finally glancing over at her from shadowed eyes. "He made two mistakes."

"Lord Micrey?" Brice asked, avoiding his gaze.

"Yes." Darius continued to watch her face. Brice was not sure what he was looking for. "He chose the wrong son and the wrong method. Jenran knows his sons too well to believe the set up."

Silence hung between them and Brice knew he was waiting for her to ask for more. Deciding he could wait, she started to cut the heavy gray fabric roughly a foot above the hem. The cloak was still going to be overlong on her, but it would no longer drag on the ground.

"That is still going to be long," he commented.

She glanced up, but still avoided those dark eyes. "I know." Then, she returned her attention to her work.

"He would never have forced the marriage." He spoke softly and thoughtfully. "He would have taken care of the daughter and child, but he could not afford to let them roam free. A rogue heir is too dangerous."

"So they would have been slaves." She set aside the scissors and began to prepare the needle.

"No." Darius's eyes followed her motions. "There is a stronghold in northern Braulyn near the Sardmarian border where the Braulian kings have kept their worst secrets safely hidden. Gwendolyn and child would have lived there in great comfort until the king could find use for them." He paused. "They would have been captives, but not slaves."

"See." Timothy's voice came clearly through the darkness, making Brice jump and drop the needle. "Ewian is not eating with us tonight. Darius captured a woman and married her just like I told you. Can I have my dinner now?"

Carefully searching through the folds of cloth on her

knees, Brice tried to catch the needle before it reached the ground.

"Alright boy," a new voice said, followed by the sounds of burdens being exchanged. Brice spotted a glimmer of silver in the firelight.

"Supplies low?" Darius asked someone as she plucked the needle from the depths of a fold. Brice looked up to find the newcomer staring at her with wide dark eyes.

"We had to leave one of the food wagons behind, so I am rationing all the meals." The man answered without taking his eyes off her. Brice was starting to feel extremely uncomfortable. His gaze was unreadable in the flickering light and she was unsure of his thoughts. "Who is the girl?"

"Brice." Darius rose and offered her his hand. Deciding it was better to rise and decrease a little of the distance between her head and everyone else's, Brice accepted it. Darius helped her up and then used his grip to pull her against his side. Suddenly, she was engulfed in his cloak; his arm pressed her against his leather jerkin. "I wish to introduce you to Hameal. He is the camp cook."

Hameal bowed with a flare of his arm. "It is a pleasure to meet you, madam." His eyes went to Darius' face and he grinned. "We all thought Darius would never take a woman. I wish you luck." Turning he called over his shoulder, "You will need it." Then he disappeared into the night.

Darius felt Brice shiver. The night air was colder than usual for early fall. Even with a quilt and heavy blanket, she still shivered in her sleep. It did not help that they were sleeping on a pallet spread on the dirt floor of the tent. She had requested they not sleep on the cot. She said she was afraid she would fall off. Darius suspected it was because she was not comfortable with him yet.

Darius watched her stir again. This time she carried the quilt with her as she rolled, exposing her back to the night. Deciding he had let her suffer enough, Darius moved over and lay closer to her. Back to back, he pulled her blanket over them both and spread his own on top. Adjusting his pillow, he settled in on his side and then waited to see what she would do. Initially, the thin body at his back was as stiff as the ground beneath them. He had a feeling she would have gotten up, but she was too cold. Slowly, the tension eased and eventually her breathing grew regular and deep with sleep. Once he was sure she slept, Darius carefully rolled over and gathered her into his arms. Her cheek was still cold when he brushed it with a finger. *She needs the warmth*, he told himself. As if agreeing, she shifted closer and uttered a soft sigh in her sleep.

Part III

"He wants to do what?" Darius' voice was low, but Brice knew instantly he was upset. Pulling on her other shoe, she scrambled to exit the tent. If Darius was angry, she did not want to be missing when it was time to leave.

"His majesty wishes to travel ahead." She heard another male voice reply in dry tones. "He is concerned for his wife. Ever since we found out that the whole Micrey thing was a ruse, he has been worried about the possibility of a coup during his absence."

Stepping into the early morning light, Brice blinked and located the two men. Darius' bent head was a foot above his companion's. The older man, whom Brice was sure she had not seen before, was only an inch or two taller than her, but made up for his lack of height in breadth. He was solid and sturdy, but not fat.

"As his personal bodyguard, you are to accompany him." The stranger stated pointedly. As if he should not have to remind Darius of his duty. "He wishes to leave immediately."

"Larer, I am not debating whether or not to accompany His Majesty," Darius informed him. Turning his head and looking straight at Brice, Darius studied her face. "I am still concerned about the wisdom of heading off without the army and I am not sure if she should come too."

Larer followed Darius' gaze to Brice. Surprise flickered behind his pale blue eyes. "And she is...?" He asked suggestively.

"My wife," Darius said firmly. "She is coming with me." That decision made, the mercenary turned and yelled, "Timothy, get your sorry hide over here." Turning back to Larer, who was still standing there a bit stunned, he ordered, "Tell the king we will be with him in a half-hour's time."

Brice could not help feeling as shocked as the man looked. What did he mean she was going with him?

The boy was slow. Darius knew it was because he did not agree with the decision. "She goes, but I am left tending the supplies." He could still hear Timothy's protest in his ears. After a brief roaring match, during which Brice made herself scarce, the boy finally began to separate the supplies that were needed for Darius and Brice to travel on their own. Leaving Timothy to his deliberately sluggish movements, Darius began looking for Brice.

She was not far. He found her huddled on the cot in their tent. She had finished dressing and even donned her cloak. "We are leaving in a moment." He crossed to gather the sack that held his gear. "You should fetch your belongings."

She did not raise her head from her knees. "I have everything."

"Then come." Darius slung the burden over his shoulder and settled the strap. "We need to fetch the horse." She looked at him from over her folded arms. He offered his hand and she looked at it like it was a suspicious looking snake. "You should know by now that I will not harm you, Brice." He waited for her gaze to rise to his. Eventually she did regard him cautiously through a film of unshed tears. Darius waited and watched her eyes. Their green depths were clear and he could almost see her balancing options. "The King is waiting." He reminded her softly. She dropped her

41

face again and took his hand.

Darius thought about their exchange for the rest of the morning and shortly after stopping for lunch, he asked, "Why do you fear me?"

Brice instantly stiffened within the circle of his arm. Repeating his habit, developed over the past few days, the stallion beneath them protested. "You really must not do that, little bird." Darius reached to catch the reins with both hands; he did not want the animal to start a charge. The moment he released her waist, Brice grabbed at his arm for balance.

"Please don't," she begged.

"Then don't stiffen every time I speak to you." He adjusted his one-handed grip on the leads and then returned his arm to her waist. "I will not let you fall," he reassured her. "Now are you going to answer my question?" He looked ahead to check on the king's position and their surroundings as he waited for her reply.

"I have no reason not to fear you."

"Did you fear your master, Lord Micrey?"

"Aye," she said, after a pause.

"And your master before him?" He probed.

"I had no master before him."

"Did he beat you?" Darius formed the words carefully. He wanted none of his contempt at the thought to creep into his voice. He had already noticed the way she shied away from any show of emotion on his part.

"Aye." The answer was so soft Darius almost missed the sound.

"Have I beaten you or hurt you in any way?"

"No…not yet." She rushed on to explain. "I have not displeased you yet."

"I promise never to beat you." He squeezed her waist. "Even if you displease me or even hurt me."

"Thank you." Her voice made it clear she still had strong doubts. Darius slowly realized how long it was going to take for him to earn her trust. Too many men had abused her and destroyed any faith she might have had.

"Why did you hunt me?" Her voice trembled, but question was clear. Drawing a deep breath, Darius tried to formulate an answer she would understand.

"I…" He never had the chance to finish the sentence.

"Ambush!" The cry came from the rear guard and instantly Darius turned. With a sharp tug at the reins, he brought the stallion around and searched the area for the king. King Jenran was about twenty-five feet to his left and closer to the rear than Darius wished. Spurring the horse forward, he maneuvered so he and Brice were between the King and the oncoming enemy.

Brice shrunk back against his body and reached to grasp anything she could to keep herself on the horse. She seemed to be managing well enough, but she would be better behind him. "You are going around behind me," Darius warned her. "Bring up your leg."

She obediently brought her leg over the horse's head. Swinging her around, he helped her to straddle the horse behind him. Not even waiting until she settled, Darius reached for his sword in the saddle scabbard. Two arms wrapped themselves around his ribs and a small body pressed against his back. *Good. She is on.* Hefting the weapon before him, he turned to face the attack.

The others were doing the same. One hundred strong, they were by no means an army, but the king had chosen his best. They would not go down easily. Darius let the others go ahead. He had two people to protect and for the girl's sake, he needed to be the last resort, not the first.

Brice pressed her face against the broad back before her and closed her eyes. The horse reared and she almost screamed as the world turned sideways. Thankfully, her grip on Darius held firm. Then, just as suddenly, the universe righted with a teeth-jarring thud. There was yelling all around them and she could pick out the king's and Ewian's voices behind them, but Darius remained silent.

An ear splitting war cry broke forth right next to them and Darius moved. Reaching back to their left, he swung at something and the yell stopped in a gurgle. Something screamed farther off and it took a moment for Brice to realize it was a horse.

Pulling their horse around in a full circle, Darius appeared to be looking for someone. Brice also looked but could not see much beyond his shoulder and sword arm. He must have spotted his object, for the horse came to a stop and Darius appeared to be looking off to their right. Turning the horse's head in that direction, they started forward. His arm and sword were in constant motion and the progress was slow. Again and again an enemy rose up to challenge them. Every one fell in a matter of moments. Right after a particularly bloody confrontation, the horse stopped moving forward. Darius tensed, so Brice prepared herself for another attack and more sudden movement. Instead, he stopped moving completely and the ruckus around them died down.

"If anyone moves, the king dies." A ragged voice announced into the sudden hush. Every muscle in Darius' back was coiled and ready for action.

"Loosen your grip, Brice," he whispered. Carefully, she obeyed. Brice realized what he was going to do the moment he moved. Using the horse as a springboard, he launched himself into the air. He landed short of his goal, but the distraction of his action gave the king and his closest bodyguard the opening they needed. King Jenran wrestled the assassin's knife from his neck and Ewian drove his blade up into the wretch's back.

Meanwhile, Darius landed and took out three men while they watched the death of their comrade. Brice found herself yelling a warning as a fourth man turned to attack Darius while he was still finishing his third opponent. Just in time, Darius turned and brought up his sword to block a blow to his head.

Brice did not see the end of that exchange, because she was forced to defend herself. Seeing the horse standing

44

calmly and a female perched upon it, one of the enemy decided to take advantage of the chaos to claim this unusual prize.

A few moments later, Darius thought someone had called his name. The voice was distressed and as he turned, his battle-crazed mind registered that it had sounded sort of like Brice. Searching the battleground quickly with his eyes, he realized she and his horse were not where he had left them moments before. Raising his sword to block his opponent's blade he spared a glance toward Jenran. The king was well defended. During the next opening, he noticed that very few of the king's men were still engaged and their group was reassembling, clearly the victors. Bringing his opponent to his knees, Darius left him. Making his way toward the edge of the battleground, he encountered Ewian.

"Did you see Brice?" he asked.

The other Ratharian looked up, surprised. "No, is she missing?"

"She and my horse disappeared." Internally, Darius winced at the foolish sound of the statement.

"A horse and rider entered the woods in that direction a minute ago," a fellow soldier offered. "I only noticed because someone was pursing them on foot."

Nodding his understanding, Darius immediately started in the direction the warrior had pointed. Brice was not a horsewoman and as intelligent as his stallion was, they were no match for anyone with experience.

"I am with you," Ewian announced as he fell into step with him. Darius threw a questioning glance his way. "I like the girl and two is better than one," He answered.

Darius was thankful for his company when they entered the first clearing beyond the trees. The stallion was backed into a corner. Hedged in on all sides by thorn bushes taller than his head, the beast was pawing the ground and obviously debating whether or not to charge the human obstacle blocking the only opening. Brice clung to his back and watched the man with the sword with even more fear than the horse. Her cloak was gone.

"Everything will be fine, my pretty," the scruffy man crooned in a rough voice. "Just stay calm and hold him until I get close enough to grab him." The man took a step forward. The horse reared with a loud whinny and dumped his rider. Then he charged the assailant, who dove for cover.

Darius ignored the horse, left the man to Ewian, and immediately ran to the fallen rider. She lay sprawled on the ground. As he approached, he tried to recall if he had seen her roll on impact or not. If she had, her injuries would be less. Her face was turned away from him and her hair fell wildly about her head. She did not move and even as he touched her, he feared the worse. Weaving his fingers through the dark curls, he found her neck and a pulse. *She lives.* Suddenly finding he could breathe again, Darius ran his eyes over the rest of her to see if there were any breaks he could find.

"The man is gone," Ewian announced from above him. "The coward ran at the sight of you. He did not much like the sight of me either, for that matter. He seems to have a fear of Ratharians."

"Many do." Darius heard his own voice reply. "We are going to need the healer; she is unconscious."

"I will fetch him." Darius barely noticed the sound of Ewian's retreating footfalls.

Brushing her hair away, Darius examined her face. A dark bruise was developing above her right eye and there were scratches on her cheeks from the branches when the horse had rushed through the trees. She was lucky she had not been knocked off by a limb. *What if she does not wake?* The thought scared him. He had only just begun to earn her trust and now he had lost her. Refusing to let the idea rest, he gently touched her head without moving it and began searching it for other injuries. Then she moaned and stirred.

Pain! Waves of it washed over her and her head felt like it was going to explode. Brice slowly became aware of the rest of her body and rapidly regretted the discovery. Every bone and joint hurt.

"Brice." A warm male voice tinged with an accent spoke from somewhere above her. Turning her head toward the sound, pain erupted behind her eyes. Taking a sharp breath of air, she realized yet another agony as her chest screamed at the motion. She must have cried out at the pain for the voice spoke again, "Hush, little bird, hush." Large hands enclosed her ribs and began carefully outlining each with their fingertips. "No," the man decided, "None are broken."

"Brice." One of the hands touched the side of her face. She had a strong feeling she knew the name of the man, but she was too tired to think now, too sleepy. "Brice," the voice insisted. "Open your eyes."

Slowly she obeyed and instantly regretted it. The world outside was bright and it increased the throbbing behind her eyes.

"Good," the voice encouraged. "Now keep them open until the healer comes. That fall might have done some serious damage." Ever so slowly, Brice focused her eyes on his face. *Darius.* She smiled. How could she have forgotten Darius? He loomed over her like a dark thundercloud. Her brain told her she should feel fear at being so helpless and at his mercy, but strangely, she did not.

"Brice." Darius' voice interrupted her thoughts. "I need you to work with me." She turned her head very slowly until she could meet his eyes. He was kneeling at her side. Once her eyes were on his face, he asked, "Can you move your legs?"

"I can feel them." She closed her eyes, concentrated, and willed her legs to move. Pain shot up her left leg and her ankle throbbed, but they moved. "I think my ankle is twisted."

"I brought the healer," Ewian announced from the other side of the clearing.

Darius slowly rose from his knees and turned to greet

the man still out of Brice's vision. "I have not moved her," Darius informed the healer. "She has struck her head, bruised her ribs, and possibly sprained her ankle."

"How many times do I have to tell you, Darius?" A short older man came to stand at her side across from Darius. "I like my job and I cannot keep it if you keep diagnosing my patients. Now shoo." Waving a hand at the two warriors, he looked down and smiled at her. Brice found herself smiling back despite the pounding in her head and the dull ache that hummed through the rest of her. "Now, you must be Brice. I am Kurt."

In under a half hour, they were on the road again. Brice was perched once again in front of Darius, but his arm was even looser than before because of her ribs. He also was keeping the pace extra slow for her head's sake. Although the tonic the healer had given her kept the pain down, her head still throbbed with each step the horse took.

"Brice?" Darius' voice came from somewhere above her, but Brice did not really care. Her eyes were closed and the oblivion of sleep waited. "Brice." Darius' voice was louder and he sounded.... Brice was not sure how he sounded. Then he tightened his hold on her. The lingering pain increased into a roar in a moment and she straightened abruptly. All the muscles in her body protested causing an involuntary gasp of pain.

"You must stay awake, Brice," Darius insisted as he relaxed his arm. "If you sleep too soon, you might never awake."

"I understand," she answered. Leaning back against him again, she tried to draw her mind to something, anything but sleep. "You did not tell me why you pursued me after the siege." Again, she felt the slight tightening of his muscles as if this were difficult. After a few moments of uncomfortable silence, he finally spoke.

"I was enslaved when I was very young," he said. Brice did not understand how this connected to what she had

48

asked, but she waited. "My first master trained slave boys into warriors. Ewian and I were part of a large group he bought from a Sardmarian slaver. At the end of seven years, we were both sold into service to the King. We excelled at our work, became part of the personal guard at the King's disposal, and then bodyguards. Because of exceptional service, I was granted my freedom. That means I am paid for my service and have a right to an extra portion of the spoils after a battle. I have not exercised that right until I chose you."

He stopped and when Brice was sure he had finished, she asked, "But why me?"

He was quiet again, but Brice was beginning to realize that if she was patient, he would eventually answer. "You were alone and needed protection." He took a deep breath and shifted. Brice was distracted by the echoes of pain that the slight extra movement caused, but she was sure she heard him mutter, "It was time." Ewian crossed in front of them to reach the side of one of the men directly in front of them. Brice watched as they fell into animated conversation.

"Is Ewian still a slave?" She asked.

"No," Darius answered. "He was freed shortly before me. He earned it by saving the king's son from a foolish mistake."

"How did you gain it?" His arms were strangely comforting. If she did not keep talking and listening, she was going to doze off.

"I discovered and helped dismantle a plot to kill the king. Enough about me," he protested. "Tell me how you got to where you were." The horse stepped slightly off causing her sore ankle to bump the side of the horse. It was a few moments before she could talk.

"I was born a slave," she said finally. "My father was the blacksmith who shoed the lord's horses, and my mother, a weaver. When I was seven, I became a handmaid and whipping girl for the lord's daughter, Gwendolyn." The man behind her stiffened, but she did not know why.

It was common practice to have a whipping boy for

noble child. Whenever the lord's son misbehaved, the whipping boy was punished, or whipped, in the noble child's presence. Brice had been told it was supposed to make the misbehaving child feel sorry for the bad deed, but she never could understand the connection. Gwendolyn had not seemed to see the connection either.

"Was Gwendolyn a well-behaved child?"

Puzzled at the question, Brice shrugged before she remembered the consequences. "I don't have anything to compare her too."

"Brice." Darius' voice was low and prodding. "How often were you whipped?"

She hesitated for a moment. "Daily," she finally managed. She was not about to tell him that some times it had been more.

"Would Lord Micrey administer the whippings?" She could hear the displeasure in his voice.

"No." Memories of Lord Micrey's drunken roaring whenever she had moved from beneath the oncoming fist flashed into Brice's head. "He did not need a reason to strike."

For a while, the only sounds were the creaking of the gear and snippets of other conversations, then Darius muttered, "Never again."

Brice would have asked him to explain, but the leader called out that it was time to stop for the night. Darius slowed their horse to a walk and guided him toward one of the trees in the center of the proposed campsite. Dismounting, he moved the saddle and Brice closed her eyes against the wave of disorientation that washed over her.

"Brice?" She opened her eyes to find Darius looking up at her with concern. "What is wrong?"

Carefully shaking her head, Brice swallowed before saying, "Just a little dizzy."

"Come." He offered her his hands to help her down. "We should eat and then have the healer check on you."

Obediently Brice leaned over and placed her hands on

his leather-covered shoulders. Sliding his right arm under her left and up along her shoulders, he instructed her to fall toward him. He then caught her legs with his left arm and brought her against his chest. Through the whole process, Brice closed her eyes against the pain, but tried not to show how much it hurt. The healer had said that her ribs were not severely damaged, but he had insisted on binding some cloth around them to support and protect in case a break had occurred.

"I am going to set you over there under that tree," Darius informed her as he began to walk. "Then I will fetch you some dinner and the healer."

"Darius is doing my job again," the healer's voice announced. Brice looked up to find him smiling warmly down at her. No trace of anger glinted in his bright eyes as he scanned her face. "He insists you have a concussion and should be kept awake for longer." He dropped his pack on the ground at her feet and squatted down so that their faces were eye-level. "I told him I would have to see for myself. So, how are you feeling?"

"How should I be feeling?" Brice was uncertain where to start.

"Does your head still hurt?"

"It went down some with the tonic you gave me, but it is starting to throb again."

Nodding his understanding, the old man opened the mouth of his sack. "I will give you more medicine for you to take right before bed. It should reduce the pain so you can sleep; now, what about your ribs?"

"Every movement hurts," Brice admitted as she remembered the traveling.

"Have you any shooting pains?" Brice shook her head and the healer smiled. "Good. I will give Darius something to bind them with later, below your clothing."

Brice felt the heat in her cheeks, but the man just kept talking. "In spite of the dizziness, your pupils are the same size and you are making complete sense. I just want to check your skull and then I will give you the medicine and leave you to your meal."

Motioning for her to lean forward, which she did, the healer removed his gloves. Running his strong sensitive fingers beneath her hair, he examined her head. He was especially interested in the lumps that had formed. "Good," he muttered.

"What is good?" Darius' voice suddenly asked from above them. Brice jumped, but the healer just pushed back on his heels and shook his head.

"How many times have I got to tell you boy." He calmly drew his riding gloves over his hands and began to pack up his sack. "I am the healer, not you."

Brice glanced up and then wished she had not. It made her head throb and Darius was looming again. He looked dark and forbidding. The man at her feet ignored him.

"Take this a half hour before you try to sleep," the healer instructed as he handed her a small vial of liquid. Then he rose. "These are for her ribs," he said as he handed Darius a roll of cloth. "Bind them firmly, but carefully."

"I have bound ribs before, Kurt," Darius responded, taking the roll.

"Let her sleep tonight." Kurt shook his finger up in Darius' face. "And if I hear about you keeping her awake all night, you will have to answer to me. Besides, if you do, she will have a headache worse than this tomorrow. Her body needs rest now, boy." He winked at Brice over his shoulder. "She is almost as hard-headed as you, but not nearly as indestructible, so be gentle." Hoisting his sack onto his back, Kurt the healer headed off in the direction of his own dinner.

Brice watched him go and waited patiently for Darius to speak.

She was so small. Darius watched her as she examined the vial in her lap. Dark brown curls had fallen out of her braid and now dangled over her forehead and neck. Her bent head hid the paleness of her face and the tightness of the skin around her eyes. She still was in pain. Settling himself on the ground at her feet, Darius rolled the bundle of material between his hands. Finally, he looked up and asked, "Have you finished your dinner?" The trencher beside her on the rock still had some bread and stew on it. She had not eaten much.

"Yes," she said; her voice was uncertain. Darius looked up again to find her eyes on his face.

"I have our tent set up over there." He gestured toward the cluster of peaked cloth roofs near the center of the glen. "I will get you some water to wash that down." He nodded toward the small glass in her hands. "Then I will put you to bed." Her eyes widened and in the instant before she dropped them, he saw fear in their depths. Unbidden, the question leapt from his mouth, "What do you fear?"

Silence fell between them and she continued to stare at the ground at her feet.

Having asked, he wanted an answer. He was curious. Taking a deep breath, he asked again. "Brice, what do you fear?"

"You." The answer was so soft, Darius was not sure he had heard her correctly. Dropping the cloths into her lap, he reached up and caught her head between his hands. Carefully forcing her look toward him, he searched her face. He had heard correctly and he was not sure what he was going to do about it. Dropping his hands, he turned and got to his feet, his mind whirling.

"I will get you that water," he announced and started toward the water supply.

Covering ground quickly, he tried to figure out the reason for his agitation. It must be because she still thought the worst of him. What Darius could not figure out is why it bothered him so much. As a Ratharian slave and then mercenary, he had long ago realized most of the people he met would believe he was some terrible beast because of his skin's darker hue. At about the same time he realized that fact, he had decided it was not going to affect how he viewed himself. He had honor and ideals just like everyone else and he lived by them and until now, that had been enough to hold the scorn and ridicule at bay.

Submerging the mug into the water in the barrel, Darius suddenly had an idea. If he completely surrounded Brice with the evidence that he was not a monster bent on manipulating and using her, she would eventually have to accept it. Carrying the now full mug before him, he purposefully started back across the encampment to where he had left his wife.

"Darius." Ewian fell into step beside him. "I have been looking for you. The King wants both of us in his tent. He has called a meeting to address strategy."

Remembering that they were due to arrive at Kiylin in two days, Darius nodded. "I will be right there. I need to move Brice to our tent. Could you find Kurt and explain that I cannot bind Brice's ribs tonight? He is going to have to."

"Sure," Ewian agreed. "Just don't dawdle. Newlywed or not, the king hates to wait." Laughing, the Ratharian turned away toward the healer's tent.

Brice was in the exact same position Darius had left her, examining her hands and the small vial in them. She looked up as he approached and offered a shaky smile in greeting. Darius lowered himself to her level and offered the mug. She swallowed the contents of the vial and immediately reached to accept the mug. While she was still drinking deeply, Darius spoke.

"The king wants me in his tent for a meeting." Her green eyes questioned him over the rim of the cup. "I sent word I was moving you to our tent before I head over. Ewian is going to tell Kurt. He should be along soon to bind your ribs before you sleep."

She lowered the cup and asked, "How long are you going to be?"

He shrugged. "The king takes whatever time he needs

and no one complains."

She nodded and offered the half-full mug back to him. "Thank you."

Quickly swallowing the rest, Darius tossed it onto the top on their supply pile. "Ready?" he asked.

Nodding, she reached up for his hand to steady herself, but Darius did not wait for her to rise to her feet. Wrapping an arm around her and one around her legs, he scooped her up and started toward the tents. Brice's only response was a startled gasp. Although Darius knew it probably would have pained her more to walk, he still felt a twinge of guilt at hurting her.

Darius set her gently, but hurriedly, on the cot in their tent. "I will send one of the men to fetch our things and deliver them here later. He will leave them outside the tent, so you will not be disturbed. The king waits," he explained and then was gone.

The sounds of camp life came through the canvas walls and filled Brice's ears, but her mind was preoccupied with Darius' earlier reaction. She was not sure how he had interpreted the emotions he had seen in her eyes, but she was certain he had not liked them.

The moment he asked her what she feared Brice's heart had jumped. She had answered honestly. She feared him. No matter how kind he was and gentle, she knew that he would turn on her some day. They all did. And when he did, she feared that the most. All that honed muscle and skill in one man, any man, was dangerous, regardless of the character of the man. Just like Lord Micrey and her father, they draw you in so you care about them and then they strike.

"Brice?"

Brice started and her body screamed, especially her ribs.

"Yes," she managed between clenched teeth. Her eyes were welling up with tears, but she refused to cry.

"May I come in?" Kurt's voice asked from outside the opening.

"Yes," she answered again, this time with less pain.

A lantern and a graying head pushed through the canvas. "He did not even leave you with a light?" Clicking his tongue at Darius' forgetfulness, the healer set his own light on the ground. Brice had been so caught up in her thoughts she had not noticed the deepening shadows.

"He was in a hurry," Brice managed through the fog she just realized was settling over her senses.

The healer examined her face closely for a moment. "Good." He smiled. "The medicine is taking effect. You will be asleep as soon as I finish." He immediately started instructing her in what he wanted her to do. Numbly Brice obeyed.

When the healer was finishing the last few circles of binding, Brice asked him suddenly, "Is Darius trustworthy?"

Tugging gently, the healer asked, "In what way do you mean?"

Swallowing back the pain that rose with the pressure, Brice clarified. "Does he ever lose his temper?"

"Yes," the man answered. "He has a violent temper when it gets the better of him, but it rarely does."

"What happens?"

The man smiled. "Everyone avoids him like the plague until it cools."

"Does he strike people, or throw things?"

Suddenly, Brice found her face being studied with great scrutiny. "Brice." Brice turned away. There was too much honesty in the healer's face. It frightened her. "No, Brice, look at me." Reluctantly Brice obeyed.

The man's eyes were dark blue and framed with wrinkles. "Darius is an unusual man. He keeps to himself for the most part, but is the truest friend any man or woman can have. I would trust him with my life before any man in this camp." He returned to the binding.

"But would he hurt me?" After the question was out, Brice wished it back. She sounded pathetic. It must be the sleep and drug induced haze closing in on her.

"All done," the healer announced and began to help her back into her clothing. As he reached for the lantern, he paused and looked back over at her. "Darius would rather die than strike you, child." Then he was gone.

Brice lay back across the cot. The medicine was strong. She did not even have the strength to lift her legs over the edge of the bed. As the darkness consumed her, she thought, *but what if he is wrong?*

"The enemy has shown itself." Trenar announced to the five other men present inside the largest tent in camp, the king's.

Darius surveyed his comrades-in-arms from his place sitting on an empty water barrel to the left of King Jenran. Koram, the head of the mercenaries and Darius' previous commander, leaned on the walking staff he used everyday. Regan, the captain of the guard, stood in the classic 'at ease' position to Darius' left. He had just come off watch duty. Trenar met Darius' eyes briefly from his position in the center of the room. He was the chief of the King's intelligence and also a former slave. Ewian stood on the opposite side of the King, watching as well. Darius had served with or under these men and respected each. If anything could be said for King Jenran, he knew how to choose the men at his back.

"I received word an hour ago that a group of about fifty men deserted the main company earlier today, roughly four hours after we left them. The men that ambushed us were not of that company, but we believe them to be in league with the deserters. For how else would they know we were coming this way?"

"So, what is to be our next move?" Koram asked.

"We are going to keep pressing onward," the king said. "If our sources are correct, Kiylin is in the control of rebels. They have taken my family hostage in the castle and are waiting for us to return."

"Do they know that we are aware they have taken Kiylin?" Regan asked.

The king looked to Trenar. "Not as far as we know, but once the deserters reach them, they will know we are suspicious."

"The reason I have called you here," Jenran explained as he straightened in his chair, "is we need to get inside the city walls. Once within, there is a chance we can wage warfare in the streets. If the citizens are willing to assist us, we can cripple the enemy until the army gets here." He left the alternative unspoken, but each of them understood the risk.

Koram readjusted his grip on his staff and leaned his head against his hands. Trenar took a seat and Ewian began to pace the small space in the center of the room.

Ewian suddenly stopped pacing. "If we ride up to the gates without acting suspiciously they might let us into the city, thinking we don't know that the city has been taken. Of course, we cannot be sure that they will. We may lose the battle before it has begun."

"Darius," Jenran said suddenly, calling everyone's attention to Darius. Even Ewian stopped his pacing to raise an eyebrow at him. "You have said nothing this evening."

"Yes," Regan smiled. "We all know you are sparing with words, but nothing? This is extreme, even for you. What is brewing?"

"I have just been thinking," Darius answered.

"That is obvious," Koram pointed out leaning forward on his stick. "Are you going to share your conclusions?"

"If we don't know our enemy," Darius said slowly, glancing pointedly in Trenar's direction. "Then I recommend we prepare for the worst and hope for the best."

Koram immediately protested. "If we approach our own gates armed to the teeth, we will be attacked first. They will know we are prepared to fight them and they will take the initiative."

Regan nodded. "Attack first; ask questions later."

Before Darius could even open his mouth to clarify, Ewian did it for him. "But they don't have to know we are armed for battle. If we just cover our weapons and keep out of any recognizable formation, they will not know we are expecting attack until after we are through the gates."

"Very good idea, but…" The king dropped off into thoughtful silence. All the rest respectfully broke off their voices. After a moment, the king said, "Darius, how is your wife doing?"

Startled at the apparent jump of topics, Darius blinked and the other men looked at the king in confusion. "Fine, Sire." Darius shrugged. "It will take time, but she will heal. Why?"

"I want her to ride in our midst tomorrow as we approach the gates. The presence of a woman among us will make us less threatening."

"Perfect," Trenar agreed. Even as the others were agreeing to the plan, Darius rose and stepped forward.

"Sire," he said. The king turned his attention back to Darius now standing conspicuously in the center of their circle.

"Yes."

"I request that Brice not be included in the approach tomorrow." Darius looked straight into his king's eyes, ignoring the other men in the room. "She was injured in the ambush because I had split responsibilities and had to choose between her and you, my king. I cannot have that happen again. Because of my lax performance, you and she almost died." Silence fell.

With trepidation, Darius watched the king think. He could be dismissed on the spot for unwillingness to perform his duties. On top of that, he was almost accepting blame for the King's close brush with death. The king could order him to go with the plan against his will. The many possible outcomes of his impulsive move rolled through Darius' thoughts as the king also pondered. None of the results were positive.

"What alternative would you suggest?" King Jenran finally asked.

Darius lowered his head to hide his surprise. "I was planning on sending her into the city ahead of us with Kurt, but if Trenar could spare a man, she could have a different companion." He regarded the king again. "Whoever went could also assess the situation and return to camp with the more information. Brice's presence would make the man appear more harmless and overlookable on the trip through the gates."

Trenar stepped forward. "I will take her, sire."

The king's dark eyes moved to the head of his intelligence. "Do you really think it will work?"

"My man has not tried to enter the gates because he would be known by the watch on duty, on the other hand." He jerked his chin toward Darius. "I could get in with the help of his wife. A peasant and his wife entering the city to visit relatives would be beneath any scrutiny."

Slowly the king nodded and it was settled. The rest of the meeting was brief and Darius wished it over. He was worried about Brice. She had been very pale and slow to respond when he had left her. It could have been the tonic the healer had given her, but....

"You are not falling asleep on us, are you?" Regan commented in a tone that made Darius wonder what he had missed. The meeting was obviously over and the group was breaking up. The King was speaking in lowered tones with Larer. The others were about to go to their separate tents.

"Leave him be," Ewian said, coming up to Darius' other side. "We are all tired and want to be home in our own beds."

"If all goes well, tomorrow night we will be." Trenar pointed out. Then easing onto his feet, he announced he was heading for his tent.

After they had taken their leave of the King, Ewian

followed Darius out into the night. "When they get into the city, have Trenar leave Brice with my wife." Ewian suggested the moment the two of them had walked beyond the hearing of the others. "Karyn will keep her safe and you will know where to find her when everything is finished."

"Thank you." Darius slowed his pace. "I must check on Brice. She was not doing very well when I left." He turned and offered his hand.

He could not see Ewian's face in the darkness, but his voice sounded understanding. Taking the offered hand, Ewian said, "We will talk tomorrow."

At about three in the morning, it began to pour rain over the camp. Dawn was just a lightening of the gray that could be seen through the steady rain. Darius peered through the tent flap at the drab morning breaking. Then he heard a sound from behind him.

Brice awoke to the steady sound of water dripping into a puddle and the drumming of rain on the oil canvas roof. The temperature of the evening before had dropped drastically. Shivering, she pulled the blanket closer to her chin. That one motion brought on a chorus of pain so loud Brice's breath caught in her chest.

She must have made a noise, for suddenly Darius was looming over her. "Brice, are you all right?" His face was in the shadow, but she could still feel the dark gray gaze fixed on her face.

Not sure she could manage to speak, she carefully nodded. The world swam, her stomach clenched, and an acidic burn bit the back of her throat. Almost as if he knew that she was not telling him the whole story, Darius moved. The sound of him rummaging came from the far corner of the tent. Brice decided it was too risky for her to follow his actions with her head. Instead she closed her eyes and wished she was dead. Just as the partial oblivion of pain laced sleep started to creep upon her, Darius was back.

"Sit up."

He has to be jesting. The thought of movement made the throbbing in her head crescendo.

"Brice." His voice was lower and if she was not so preoccupied, Brice would have been concerned about his temper. "You need to take this. Kurt ordered me to give it to you as soon as you woke." A large hand gripped her shoulder and Brice instinctively recoiled. "No." Darius' other hand prevented her from moving farther. Picking her up like she was a child, he sat on the edge of the bed and cradled her against him. Brice suddenly found her eyes open and watching him trying to open a small vial one-handed. Before she had completely registered the meaning of his words, he was pressing the cold container to her lips.

"Open, little bird," he said. His breath brushed her cheek. "It will help, I promise." Reluctantly she parted her lips. Bitter liquid filled her mouth and then a large warm hand massaged her throat. The moment she swallowed, the rim of a wider container was pressed to her lips. Obediently, she opened her mouth without prompting. Cool water flowed across her tongue carrying away some of the bitter residue.

"More?" Darius asked after she had swallowed the first mouthful.

"Yes." The thin edge returned to her lips. This time it washed away the traces.

"More?" He asked again.

Weakly, Brice tried to shake her head.

"I understand." Darius immediately stopped her attempts by catching her head beneath his chin. Setting down the container, he put her back in the bed. The now familiar fog was clouding her senses, but she was aware enough to make note of his return to bed. He tucked the covers around them both before settling against her back. She was not sure, but he might have whispered, "Goodnight, little one."

Part IV

The rain had stopped, but the air was heavy with the threat of more. Darius felt the moisture that had been collecting on his skin and clothes despite the cold. Surveying the edge of the clearing, he wiped his forehead with the back of his glove. He despised this weather. Wishing it would just rain and get it done, he spotted movement among the trees. After another moment, Brice began to come into view.

Darius cringed inwardly as he watched Brice's slow progress back up the path from the woods. Being the only woman in camp, she had the eastern side of the encampment to herself as long as she gave the sentry ample notice. As much as it bothered him, Darius found he also admired her spunk. She insisted on walking, unaided, on her own two feet. She fetched her own breakfast and returned the dishes on her own. She did not complain or even wince unless she thought no one was looking. Only last night, vulnerable and exhausted, had he seen the true extent of her trial.

She reached a fallen log on the edge of camp and sank onto it gratefully. Darius had yet to tell her the plans made the night before. She would probably be happy to leave him behind. He, on the other hand, was growing attached to his little brown bird and was not sure he wanted to have her out of his sight. Breathing deeply, he began his approach. She looked up almost immediately.

"Hello." A wobbly smile flitted across her lips but did not reach her eyes before it disappeared.

"How are you doing?" Darius was not sure he would get an honest answer, but it was worth a try.

She shrugged. "Kurt said it is going to be really hard for a few days. My ribs alone will be tender for a very long time."

Nodding, Darius glanced at the ground and crossed his arms in front of him. "There has been a change in plans since yesterday." Looking down at her, Darius met green eyes. Immediately they dropped their gaze to the ground at his feet. "I want you out of danger and the king needs to know what will be greeting us on the other side of the city walls, so we decided that you and a scout are going to enter the city this morning. He will be leaving you inside and returning with news tonight." He could see she was fidgeting with her skirt. "Ewian's wife will give you a bed until I can join you."

She said some thing that he did not catch. Squatting so that their heads were level, he asked, "What did you say?"

"How long will it be before you return?"

"If all is well, it might be only a day."

"And if not..." he felt her gaze again on his face.

"I honestly don't know," he reluctantly admitted. This time, when he met her eyes, she kept them on his face. "Karyn will supply you with anything you will need and Timothy should be arriving in a few days. I promise I will send news as soon as I can, all right?" The concern in her eyes was encouraging, but she still shied away from his hand when he reached up to stroke her cheek.

Silence fell and Darius found himself wishing he knew what she was thinking.

"When do we leave?" Her voice trembled.

"Immediately." Pushing up to full height, he offered her his hand. "Trenar is bringing the horses. I am going with you as far as possible. We want to cut the walking distance as much as we safely can." She accepted his assistance and

64

carefully rose. Drawing her toward the horses, he said, "Come, let me introduce you to Trenar."

A large drop of water landed on Brice's eyelid. She jumped and instantaneously the arm around her waist tightened. The horse plodded on undisturbed. He was getting used to her sudden movements. Ahead of her, past the bobbing head of the horse, she could see Trenar on the back of a second horse. A stray drop must have also hit him for he was carefully lifting the hood of his dark brown cloak. Three more splashes of water and Brice began to think about doing the same. Darius beat her to it.

"Can you still see?" he asked as the fabric enclosed the back of her head and dipped into her line of vision.

"Yes, thank you," she answered.

The silence broken, Darius seemed encouraged to fill it. "I think you will like Karyn. She is strong and feisty. A lot like you." Brice was so surprised that Darius thought she was strong she almost missed his next few words. "She will welcome your company. Spending all her time with little ones makes her hunger for adult companionship."

"Ewian has children?" Brice tried, but could not manage to picture the large barbaric warrior with one child, let alone more.

"Yes, three." There was a smile in his voice. Then, he changed the subject. "You can tell Karyn anything you want, she can be trusted, but do not tell anyone else anything."

Solemnly Brice nodded.

"The deep forest ends soon and I am going to have to leave you and Trenar." Brice felt panic tighten her throat. As much as she was not completely sure she trusted Darius, he was the only constant thing in her life right now. The arm around her middle was gradually tightening. "Do what he tells you, all right?"

He is worried, she suddenly realized.

Again, she nodded. Laying her hand over the arm around her, Brice tried to understand the strange new sensation that overwhelmed her fear. He was concerned and it comforted her.

Almost on cue, Trenar drew back on the reins and came to a stop. Darius followed suit. Dismounting in one clean movement, Trenar turned and caught the bridle of their mount. Darius descended first and turned to help her down. Without being asked, she reached out for his shoulders. He lifted her down as he normally did, but did not immediately release her. Instead, he pulled her closer. Surprised, Brice raised her head to protest but found the words died before they reached her tongue.

Darius caught her lips with his. *What does he think he is doing?* The thought was brief and fleeting because before she knew it she was standing breathless and alone. Vaguely she heard Darius' voice addressing Trenar close by.

"Tell Karyn that I will send Timothy as soon as I can," he told Trenar. As she turned toward them and the horse stepped sideways, Brice glimpsed the end of a brief handshake. Walking back toward her, he gathered the horses' reins as he came. Stopping again before her, he smiled down at her. His eyes were dark beneath the shadow of his hood. "Goodbye, little bird." Then bowing his head, he strode off into the brush.

"We should start." Trenar suggested. Numbly Brice watched him pull his hood down so that only his thick beard showed. "Tuck in your hair and slump your shoulders," he ordered before starting toward the thinning trees.

Obediently, she followed.

Time passed in a blur of pain and a slight fog. As the medications that Kurt had given her worked their way out of her system, Brice's mind progressively quickened, but at the same rate so did the pain. She was still sore. Vaguely noting that they were following a main road, she kept her eyes on the ground appearing from beneath Trenar's feet. Darius' strange actions were more than enough to occupy her mind.

They reached the gates of the city right as it began to downpour. The soldiers, not wanting to stand out and get soaked, were posted under the shadow of the arch. The entering travelers plodded past them for inspection. Occasionally someone was pulled aside for questioning, but it appeared that no unusual care was being taken. Trenar and Brice trudged past without incident.

The city was crowded in spite of the rain and the mud in the streets. Brice found herself so involved in keeping track of Trenar and avoiding collisions, she had no energy to look at her surroundings. Feeling harassed and claustrophobic, she was extremely thankful when Trenar turned off the main street into a quieter neighborhood. The rain slowed and tapered off to nothing.

The houses lining the street were nicer than she had ever seen. Moving more quickly, Trenar strode along purposely. Brice had to speed up to a hasty trot to keep up. Although he was not as tall as Darius, her guide was still taller and longer limbed than her. He increased the pace now that they were unhindered by a crowd. At the end of the street, a high wall blocked the way and there appeared to be no way to turn.

They came to a hasty stop and Brice's knees almost gave out. For the first time in hours, Trenar spoke. "Are you going to make it?" His voice was rough, but not unkind.

"Rest." She gasped. "Please." Her ribs were throbbing. Gingerly, she eased to the ground. The cobblestones were far from comfortable, but she needed to get off her shaky legs. Her head throbbed and she was sure her healing ankle was swollen. Closing her eyes against the painfully dim daylight, she tried to push away the cold. It was a doomed endeavor though. Freezing water was seeping into her skirts from the street beneath her.

Kneeling next to her, Trenar examined her face. He did not remove his hood, but he did lift it enough so she could see that his eyes were blue and worried. "You are doing a great job," he said encouragingly. "We are practically there. Do you think you can continue with my help?"

She took a deep breath and nodded. He immediately rose and offered her his hand. Taking it, she found herself being pulled to her feet. With his arm supporting her beneath her shoulders and around her ribs, they approached the wall. Brice winched at every step, but together they waded through the waterlogged brush at the base. Off to the left, Trenar directed her along the wall and behind a stand of bushes and an ancient tree. There, blocked from the view of the street, was a door. About five feet high and two feet wide, it was set back into the thick stone of the wall and almost impossible to see from the side.

Trenar produced a key from somewhere and thrust it into the lock. With a quick turn and a muted click, the latch released and the door swung inward. In moments, they were through and he was locking it again from the other side.

"Remind me to give this to Karyn," Trenar said before making the key disappear into his jerkin.

"Why would Karyn want the key?" Brice asked.

"This is their property," Trenar stated matter-of-factly. "Come." He offered an arm and Brice took it gratefully. "It is time for me to introduce you."

Beyond the trees guarding the small door, a large walled yard spread out. The house, a ways from the back wall, was a simple building with three windows overlooking the garden: one on the second floor and two on the first. As they approached the first row of vegetables, a small figure dashed past them up the path to the door of the house. Brice glimpsed what she thought was a flash of red as it disappeared inside, but she was not sure.

"We are being announced," Trenar commented with an amused smile.

Just as he spoke, the door opened again and a medium-sized woman emerged with a child behind her. The woman and child both had red hair. Certain that Trenar had gotten the wrong house, Brice slowed her steps.

"Ah, Trenar." The woman smiled, but as she approached, Brice saw fear in the woman's eyes. "Where have you harkened from?" Not waiting for an answer, she continued. "Come in and rest a bit. You can test some of Joyla's first loaf of bread."

"Sounds wonderful," Trenar replied with a similar false lightness. "How are the girls these days?" They were almost to the door now.

"They are all healthy and well." Their hostess stepped aside so they could enter the house. Brice's numb feet stumbled on the first step, but Trenar, by sheer strength, all but dragged her into the building. "Joyla is becoming quite a little lady." The woman said before she followed them inside.

The instant the door was shut, the woman's face changed. "Joyla," she called. The sound hurt Brice's ears. Trenar set her on the nearest chair as the sounds of feet came from above them.

"What are you doing here? Where is the army? Why aren't you with them?" The woman asked. Brice was still certain that she could not be Karyn. She looked up to find their hostess glaring at Trenar.

"Calm down, Karyn. Ewian was perfectly fine when I left him this morning. A contingent of the army is just miles outside the walls. We were not certain about the reception awaiting us inside the city. I was sent to scout things out and Darius sent Brice with me." Trenar began removing his cloak. The fabric was water logged and dripping on the packed dirt floor. "He wants you to take care of her until he returns. She is his wife." Karyn nodded her head in Brice's direction and turned immediately back to Trenar.

Another redheaded child had appeared suddenly. Brice judged her to be about ten. The child's face left no further doubt in Brice's mind about the father. She had Ewian's dark brown, almost black, eyes.

Turning to the older child, Karyn said, "Joyla, get out
the bread and cheese in the pantry, Uncle Trenar and his friend
are hungry." She took Trenar's cloak and waited for his boots.

Brice rose and started to remove her own cloak while
Karyn and Trenar continued their discussion.

"Since when has Darius been married?" Karyn asked
as the man pulled of his second boot.

Sitting down on the bench by the door, Trenar sighed.
"Since right after Lord Micrey was defeated. I suggest you
keep your questions to those that Brice cannot answer because
I am going to be leaving almost immediately."

"But you will have to wait for these to dry at least."
She raised the sopping garment for emphasis, showering her
own skirts anew.

"I was hoping that you would lend me one of Ewian's.
I really need to hurry. I have lost time already and need to
return to camp by nightfall." The eldest girl was setting the
food on the table and Trenar eyed it hungrily.

"Very well." Karyn briskly turned and collected
Brice's cloak and headed toward the fireplace. Spotting her
younger daughter watching from the side, she told her, "Lysa,
fetch your father's extra cloak from the trunk in the bedroom."
Lysa disappeared through a door to the left of the fireplace.

Karyn spread out the wraps in front of the fire. "The
least I can do is feed you and tell you what I know," she said
as she turned toward the oven set in the wall next to the
fireplace.

"That would be helpful," Trenar admitted. "What is
the latest news from the castle?" He leaned back in his chair.

After trying to follow the conversation, Brice soon
found her head getting heavy and her stomach tightening in
response to the smells of cooking food. The whole time that
Karyn was enlightening Trenar, she was producing a large
selection of food from various nooks in the kitchen. Finally,
she paused after setting a steaming loaf of fresh bread on the
large table and announced they could come to the table to eat.

Trenar rose and complemented Joyla on the golden colored loaf.

Brice did not catch the rest of the following exchange; instead, she concentrated on rising again. After the brief rest, her muscles had decided they had taken enough abuse and were not going to cooperate. As she gradually managed to gain her feet, Karyn exclaimed, "Trenar, why didn't you say she was injured!"

In a flurry of activity, Brice found herself being ushered carefully up the stairs behind the fireplace onto the second floor. Dimly aware of a large room and four beds of varying sizes, Brice was directed to the largest. "Joyla, fetch my nightdress."

Karyn made Brice sit on the edge of the bed while she removed her shoes. Once Trenar had been shooed back down to the kitchen, Karyn helped Brice out of her wet clothing and into a dry gown. Brice found she had no strength to protest and meekly obeyed every command. This was good because Karyn was not one to listen to any objections. In the end, she and Joyla left her tucked snugly into bed to sleep until Karyn could bring up some sustenance appropriate for a weak stomach. Brice wanted to point out there was nothing wrong with her stomach, but lacked the initiative. The bed was too soft and her bones too weary. Sleep claimed her almost the instant the hatch closed.

Darius glanced restlessly at the sky. The gray expanse gave not one hint as to the time that had passed. "Will you stop worrying?" Ewian hissed. Darius dropped his attention to the battle plans he was supposed to be studying and ignored his friend. That did not discourage Ewian. "You are worrying too much," Ewian accused as he whipped the rough map from beneath Darius' nose.

"Trenar is not back yet," Darius pointed out, "and the army should have caught up with us by now. Especially considering all the time we lost with the attack and having to slow down for the wounded. I am concerned about what might be keeping him."

"Trenar has not had time to do more than get his bearings," Ewian protested.

Darius was about to comment, but one of the sentries was approaching.

"There is movement of some kind to the west of us. It looked like a group of thirty to thirty-five armed men heading toward the city." The man informed Darius as he snapped to attention.

"What kind of men?" Ewian asked as Darius returned the salute.

"They are armed and in a hurry for some reason we cannot identify. They are not part of our army or any other that we know."

Darius caught Ewian's intrigued glance and dismissed the soldier with a nod. Ewian immediately started to roll up the maps before them. "The king should be in his quarters about now," Darius commented as he reached for the battle plans that they had worked out so far.

Ewian nodded. "He will want to know about this." Grimacing slightly, he paused and glanced at Darius. "This means we are probably going to make our move tomorrow morning with or without Trenar's report."

"I only hope he figures out the change in plans in time to help," Darius said. Together they headed across camp to inform the king.

Brice slept for an entire day. Except for the interruptions of meals, she was oblivious to the passing of time. In the following afternoon, Brice awoke to silence. There was a large metal wash tub at the end of her bed with two towels draped over the end. Feeling sore from laying so long in one spot, Brice pushed herself up onto her elbows and looked around the room for the first time.

The room covered the whole second floor. Three smaller beds stood against the other outside walls, each with a chest at the foot. The bed she had been occupying for the past day was wide enough for two people to sleep side by side. The two windows on the tallest walls of the room were covered with dark curtains that dimmed the bright sunshine beyond.

Carefully she eased her feet over the edge of the bed. Just as they touched the rough surface of the floorboards, Karyn appeared in the stairwell at the far end of the room. Catching sight of Brice, she smiled. "Feeling better?" she asked.

Brice nodded and eyed the steaming bowl in her hands that had just come into sight. Her stomach rumbled loudly and she suddenly smiled. It was anxious for sustenance. Karyn smiled in return. "Here." She crossed the room and offered the bowl cradled in a cloth nest to Brice. "You eat this and I will start carrying up bath water for you." The matron immediately disappeared down the stairs again. Obediently, Brice started in on the stew.

After she finished the soup, it took her an hour to scrub herself. It had been many weeks since she had been allowed to bathe. While the castle was under siege, the water supply had been just as short as the food supply. Since then, there had been no time. Brice found herself reveling in the feeling of clean skin and hair. It had been too long.

As she dressed in her much cleaner old clothing, she found herself wondering what Darius would think of her now. Without the smell of sweat and dirt, she might actually please him. She fixed her tunic so that white place where her slave collar had been was not obvious, but Karyn still commented on it when Brice appeared in the kitchen.

"So you are a former slave." Karyn set a plate with bread and cheese on the table in front of Brice and then went to pick up the crying baby from the small raised chair at the end of the table. "Once being a slave himself, Darius can be pretty touchy about the issue." As she wiped the child's face and hands, she sat down on the far side of the table. "How are you feeling?"

Brice, who had been watching her hostess making quick work of cleaning the cereal coated baby, found it difficult to speak. Dropping her eyes, she examined the bread before her. "Better, thank you."

"Good." Karyn rose and setting the little one on the floor, she turned to the hearth. "Trenar was not exactly clear on what happened, but I gathered you had been injured in the last skirmish and were still recovering." Moving to the hearth, she inspected the contents of the large pot hanging directly over the flames and then the bowl sitting close by with a towel over it. "So how did you and Darius end up married?"

Brice watched as Karyn went over to a large wooden cupboard and brought out a flour sack. She wondered how she was going to explain something she did not even understand. Karyn set the sack down on the sturdy table with a thud and small clouds of flour wafted across the wooden surface. She took a handful of flour out of the bag and began to sprinkle it across the table.

Finally, Brice spoke. "The siege broke, my master was killed and I was trying to get away when Darius caught me." She could still remember the terror and urgency to run and hide. The almost paralyzing fear that someone would catch her was only a thought away. She shivered. "He promised to help me, but I had to do exactly what he said."

Karyn nodded and a red curl came loose from her knot. Brushing it back behind her ear with an impatient movement, she turned again to the hearth. "That sounds like Darius." Picking up the large clay bowl, she brought if to the table. "He gets bossy and overbearing, but he does know how to get things done. So, you were almost part of the spoils?"

Brice could not manage to meet Karyn's eyes. "Yes, I guess so."

"So, when did the marriage happen?" Karyn dumped a large mound of dough out of the bowl and onto the flour-strewn table.

"As soon as we got to their camp." Brice picked at the bread. "He insisted it was the only way to keep me safe."

As Karyn began kneading the dough, a small hand explored Brice's ankle. When she glanced down, Brice found a pair of bright green eyes regarding her solemnly from under the table. Karyn spoke, "He was right. The women left undefended after a city or castle falls are considered part of the reward for the victor. But as much as he is right, he was pressuring you. Ewian tries similar tactics with me, but he seldom gets away with it." The child below the table lifted her arms to be picked up. Reluctantly, Brice complied, gritting her teeth against the resulting pain in her ribs.

"How do you get him to stop without getting beaten?" Brice asked as she settled the sturdy little girl in her lap. The girl pulled at Brice's sleeve and began to sing to herself.

"What do you mean, beaten?" Karyn asked in a shocked voice. "Has that man hit you?" She had stopped kneading and was regarding Brice with a mixture of horror and disbelief on her face. "I have never known Darius to harm a woman in his life."

"He hasn't hit me." Brice hurried to clarify. "But…" She was not sure. He was so big and powerful. Every other man she had ever known had beaten their wife or child regularly. Was it possible that this man did not?

"But what?" Karyn had resumed the kneading and reached into the bag for some more flour for the table. "Listen to me, girl. These men have been on the receiving end of enough beatings to know how it is. That is why I trust Ewian to never try something like that with me. There is also the fact he loves me, but that is beside the point. He has been a slave and knows first hand about the humiliation and frustration." She turned to wash her hands. "Do you think I would willingly marry the man and have children with him if he was not trustworthy?" Her dark red brows were drawn together and the green eyes were sparkling as she looked back over her shoulder at Brice.

Brice was surprised at the woman's reaction. "I did not know you had a choice," she murmured quietly.

"Yes, I had a choice." Karyn dried her hands and then lifted a pan off a nearby hook. "Didn't you?" Setting the pan on the table, she started to form loaves. Brice watched her fingers coaxing the dough into smooth lumps the perfect size for the compartments in the metal sheet.

Darius had given her a choice in the garden, sort of. He had given her a choice right before they were married. Of course, the alternatives to both decisions would have been painful and he had been extremely clear about what he wanted her to choose, but he had still given her a choice. Finally, as the last lump settled into the pan, Brice admitted, "Yes, I had a choice."

Karyn's hands stilled and Brice looked up at her face. She was watching her with a thoughtful look on her face. "He will give you choices, Brice. And if you let him, I would venture to guess he will love you. He is a good man." Then, she smiled warmly. "I am happy he has finally married and given me a companion." Lifting the pan and turning to open the oven door, she declared. "When I am through, you will know how to be a good soldier's wife."

Brice was surprised to find she actually wanted to try.

The sky was just turning rosy above the trees. As Ewian had predicted, they were about to make their move. Darius glanced around for the fifth time in so many minutes. Scattered about the King in a pattern that at first glance did not appear planned were four others besides him. The rest of their small army was similarly arranged in random groups and trying to act casual.

Ewian caught his eye but his face remained impassive. Earlier, they had agreed that they were not pleased with how the situation looked. Darius hated letting the king walk in with them. But their company was small and they needed every man and more. According to the message that had arrived during the night, the main army was roughly four hours behind them. So close, but too far. He only hoped they appeared in time. At least their current group had only to hold out until then.

The signal was given and they began to move. Keeping the King within his sight, Darius readjusted his grip on the reins and focused on the walls coming into view. For the fiftieth time in the past hour, he mentally ran down his gear and its careful placement on him and his horse. His mail lay heavy beneath his leather and metal jerkin. His heavy cloak concealed the dagger in his belt and his shield was carefully attached to the travel gear behind him to hide the hilt of his sword within easy reach. Looking around casually, he tried to relax and prepare his mind for the madness to come.

He found himself thinking of Brice. If all was well, she was safely with Karyn and the children. She was protected by strong walls and Ewian's wife's knowledge of how to protect her family in this type of situation. As much as he missed her presence, he knew she was safer inside the castle and city walls. Now he would be free to defend his master and king without the distraction of protecting her and worrying that his failure might bring her death. Somehow the thought of her death caused him more dread than that of his king or himself. The fact he did not fear his death did not surprise him. He had been facing the possibility of his life ending in the next instant for all of his days. As soldier and bodyguard, he had been entrusted with other men's lives more times than he could count, but never had one life been so much more important than the others. Disturbed by the course of his thoughts, Darius broke them off.

All he could hear was the creaking of leather and metal and the heavy plodding of horseshoes on grass and dirt. Some of the men started up nervous conversations. The guise of relaxed banter was good, but Darius hoped none of the men at the gates would be able to hear the actual words. The hearing of the discourse of the younger pair to his right was a dead give away that something was wrong. The men were too nervous to think straight.

"It looks like rain," the one said in a monotone.

"The clouds are certainly gray," the second replied in a strained voice that cracked on the word gray. He did not spare a glance for the clear blue sky above his head.

"Do you suppose the farmers will have a good harvest?" the first continued.

"Apples were in season last month."

Ewian edged his stallion closer to the king's. Darius turned his attention away from the nonsensical conversation. Dropping back behind the king's right flank, he scanned the top of the walls just visible beyond the trees. Not many metal helmets caught the sunlight. He wondered if that number would increase as they approached.

They rounded the last grove of trees and the walls and the entrance came into view. The short drawbridge was down, the main city gate with its large doors stood wide, and the heavy iron portcullis was raised so only the spikes showed below the arch. Darius edged closer to the king's flank. This was going too well. Something was amiss.

As they approached, there was no shout of greeting or challenge from the walls and only ten or so guardsmen were visible on the outside of the gate. Darius watched the gatehouse above the doors. That was where the large gears worked to lower and raise the portcullis. No activity or movement could be seen. The great doors of the gate opened outward so that the portcullis supported them from within when they were closed. A second set of even heavier doors could be closed on the opposite side of the portcullis so it was enclosed by the two sets.

Darius' task was to get the King through and to a meeting place of safety. They were expecting a long battle in the streets and the King needed to be able to command the men from a hidden stronghold. Darius already had a place in mind deep in the old city.

Most of the other men were instructed to scatter and build barricades in the streets. Hopefully most of the citizens would be helpful. If they were, there was a chance of success. If not, the cause was essentially doomed.

The shadow of the wall fell over them and they passed into the tight courtyard immediately inside the gate. An armed company awaited them and began to escort them toward the castle that loomed on the hill above the city. Behind them a crowd had gathered, probably citizens, their daily routine interrupted by the king's arrival. Keeping his eyes sharp, Darius looked about for the best avenue of escape. He wanted to have the king off the main street before the worst of the madness began.

Only moments before the loud boom of the portcullis closing echoed through the streets, Darius spotted the street he was seeking. Signaling the King and the rest of his circle to follow him, Darius suddenly turned his horse and plunged into the crowd. He had chosen a place where the crush was thinner so the likelihood of someone getting trampled was smaller. Reassured by the clatter of hooves behind him, he galloped down the cobblestone alley and into the cramped squalor of the old city.

Four hours later, Darius scowled as he carefully moved the leather sleeve of his jerkin over the bandage wrapping his upper arm. It still hurt. "Be careful not to start the bleeding again," Kurt cautioned. Darius grimaced in response. He had been injured often enough to know the drill.

"How long?" Darius asked as he eased the garment over the rest of him. The healer helped.

"Don't use it for a few days at least." The older man started lacing the front of the shirt.

"Kurt, do you really believe I am going to be able to do that?" Darius grimaced again as he reached for his cloak. The man was an idiot if he thought Darius was going to be able to nurse himself. They were fighting for the city and the king needed all the protection and support he could get. Half of the men were trying to get the main gate open before their reinforcements appeared and the other half were trying to get into the castle where the leaders of the rebellion had barricaded themselves in with hostages from the royal family.

The healer frowned in response. "I am aware of the circumstances, boy. I just would hate for Brice to miss out on the joy of growing old before she is widowed."

Darius paused at the thought in spite of the fact it had crossed his mind frequently in the past few hours. "The thought of dying had crossed my mind, old man. I do not consider myself invincible." Awkwardly he tried to swing his cloak across his shoulder with one hand. It fell short. "At least she would be a free widow. You know that our marriage makes her no longer a slave."

The healer caught the slipping cloth and assisted him in fastening it so it fell over his bad left arm. "I figured that was part of the reason, but widowhood is still nothing to be desired, whether one is free or not. And marriage to a one-armed mercenary is not much better." Patting Darius' right arm, Kurt looked up at him briefly. "Besides, I have grown fond of you. Now get." He shooed Darius toward the hall. "And send in the next man as you leave."

Obediently, Darius stepped into the dim and cramped passage. Two men stood next to the door, one leaning against the wall and looking quite gray. "He is waiting," he muttered before heading to the stair to the common room below.

The Falcon Claw Inn's common room was empty except for three men leaning over the table in the back corner. As Darius approached, the center man lifted his head. "If you are ready, Darius, we are to head toward the castle and find a way in. The king needs us to open the gates from the inside." Jarn's eyes challenged Darius to turn down the assignment.

"Then let us go. I know a back way in." Darius turned and headed for the door. He could hear Jarn's hurried shuffling gait as he tried to catch up. The man was a good soldier, but Darius had never gotten along easily with him. He always had an underlying tone to his voice that reeked of contempt.

Part V

Brice was helping Joyla clear the table after dinner while Karyn heated the dishwater when there was suddenly a loud banging on the front door. "I will get it." Lysa jumped up from playing with her little sister on the floor. Crossing the room at a run, the child eagerly reached for the latch. Brice glanced over to see Karyn wiping her damp hands on her apron and starting to move toward the door. A crease had appeared between her eyebrows. It must be unusual to have callers at this time of the evening. Suddenly the door opened with a loud bang as it bounced off the wall and shook the house.

Brice turned in time to see Lysa dangling from a large stranger's arm, her small face white against the dark red of her hair. "Don't move or I kill the brat." An evil looking blade lifted to hover threateningly close to the girl's throat. Brice felt the familiar burst of fear in her center. As it spread into numbness of shock, she tore her eyes up to the face of the man. Cold black eyes looked back at her and she almost shivered. This man was ice.

"Which one is Darius'?" He demanded. Three men had entered from behind him and were now surveying the room.

"The dark one." One of them pointed at her. Brice's eyes flew to his face and her heart sunk. It was the cook Darius had introduced as Hameal in camp only a few days ago. *What is going on?*

Instantly the other two moved to restrain her. The leader then addressed Karyn who still stood as if bolted to the floor. The only life in her face was the emotion in her eyes. They glared at the stranger who held her child. "We are going to take both of them. Tell Darius that if he wishes to see his wife alive again, he needs to only follow. I will be waiting."

Jerking his head toward the open doorway, he signaled for the others to leave. Brice found her arms being forced behind her. Something coarse was tightly wrapped around her wrists. One of the men shoved her forward so forcefully, she stumbled and wrenched her shoulder. Biting her lip to distract herself from the tears burning her eyes, she struggled to recover her balance. Somehow, she made it over the threshold into the falling night.

The leader, as she saw the cold one was, came out last and immediately threw Lysa in Hameal's direction. "Watch the brat," he growled. "She is almost as valuable as the wench." He strode off down the empty street. Her keeper, an older man, jabbed her hard in her still tender ribs to get her to follow. Obediently she turned and started walking, but her attention was on Lysa. The child was surprisingly silent. As they moved, Brice worriedly glanced over at her. Pale face staring woodenly before her, the child walked as if in a dream, a nightmare of the worst kind.

"This way," Darius said as he and Jarn hurried along. The familiar street of neat houses ended in a dead end. The towering outer wall of the castle grounds loomed. Darius ignored it and headed along to the left. There, as he expected, was the hidden door into Ewian's backyard. Pulling out the key, he made quick work of the lock and pushed the door inward. Ducking to enter, he turned immediately to allow Jarn

82

to follow. Closing the door behind them and locking it again, he turned to find Jarn surveying the darkening garden.

"Is this your place?" Jarn asked as they stepped from beneath the shadow that the moon cast. The leaves still remaining on the vegetables in the garden outlined shaky rows. A child's wooden toy horse lay on its side in one of the beds.

"Ewian's," Darius replied. Avoiding another toy on his way down the main path, he led the way toward the rather small building opposite the gate. "The only way onto the street is through the house." Jarn did not reply, but Darius heard his following footfalls. Turning his attention to the building, Darius had an overwhelming sensation that something was not right. Then he heard the cry. Covering the remaining distance at the run, he reached the back door and forced it open. The latch flew free of the doorframe at his first assault and skidded across the floor with a clatter and stopped a few feet into the room.

It took him only a moment to register the tear stained faces of Karyn and Ewian's eldest child, Joyla. Karyn was protectively rising to place herself between her daughter and the door. The youngest was at her feet. The baby must have been the one who had cried out, because she was now regarding Darius with an upset startled look and her face was red.

"What happened?" Darius demanded.

"Darius." Karyn gasped at the same moment and then broke down in sobs. As her mother sank to her knees wailing into her apron, Joyla ran up to Darius and flung herself at him. Instinctively Darius caught her and picked her up. Just then, Jarn arrived behind him.

"Karyn, you must calm yourself." Darius crossed to the woman. "I need to know what happened. Where is Lysa?"

Karyn lifted her face and put a great deal of effort into suppressing her sobs. "Strange men appeared and took Brice...and..." A shudder shook her. "Lysa," she whispered.

"Which way did they go?" Darius asked.

"They turned left," Joyla answered with a hiccup. "Are you going to get them?"

"I will try," Darius replied as Karyn attempted to wipe her eyes on her already damp skirts. "How long ago was this?"

"Ten minutes at most." She sniffed.

"Jarn." Darius began untangling the child's arms from around his neck.

"Here," Jarn replied from near the back door.

"Let's go," Darius declared. He handed Joyla to her mother and started for the front door.

The path that passed beneath Brice's feet changed from cobblestones to fine gravel. When it narrowed, she looked around to find them walking along a manicured garden path bordered by hedges. Her keeper had noticed her gaze and jabbed her in the ribs again. She gasped at the pain and almost doubled over. The man's grip on her bound hands propelled her forward. "Move wench," he hissed. "Or I will bruise your pretty face too." He snickered. "Ogert might do that anyway, just to annoy Darius."

"What did Darius do to him?" She asked as soon as she could manage.

"Silence!" Something hard struck her across her shoulders bringing her to her knees on the gravel. A cold metal edge pressed against her chin lifting it and the leader's icy eyes bore into hers. "Hostages speak only when asked a direct question." His voice made her want to shiver, but if she did, the blade would cut her. Clenching the muscles of her back, she prayed for strength.

Apparently satisfied that she understood, the leader withdrew the blade and started again to stride down the path. Brice had a brief glimpse of the large fortress they were approaching before being dragged to her feet again. The prodding and gloating of her keeper continued until she stumbled up wide stone steps. They passed through a large door, which Ogert barred behind them and Brice was allowed to sink to her knees once more. The cold of the entrance hall tiled floor instantly began to seep into her legs. Lysa was shoved down a short ways away and the moment the men's back were turned, she moved to Brice's side and leaned against her. Brice had not the heart to tell child that her weight was hurting her ribs. As much as she strained her ears, she could not hear the men's conversation.

After the brief whispered conference among the four, the leader strode off down one of the main halls and disappeared. Hameal ordered her and Lysa to their feet. Obediently they struggled up, but they both received a jab for good measure.

The men herded them down a long sub-corridor and up three long flights of steep stairs. Just when Brice was certain her legs were going to give out if she saw another stair, they turned off into another wider passage. Stopping before a set of great double doors, Hameal pushed in front, produced an ornate key from the purse at his waist, and opened the doors. Brice caught a glimpse of light on metal and then the cord binding her hands fell away. "Inside," he ordered before shoving Brice hard between the shoulders. Unable to keep her balance, she was propelled into the dark room and landed face first on a surprisingly soft carpet. With a cry, Lysa landed a few feet to her right. The doors were closed firmly and the latch caught. Then, with a loud hollow clunk, the bolt slid home.

Not waiting to see if Jarn followed or not, Darius started to run. Each footfall jarred his wounded arm, but he ignored it. Catching up with the kidnappers was more important. He spotted them in the Kiylin gardens. Moving from shadow to shadow he kept them in his sight only dimly aware that Jarn was following on his heels. He was surprised when they stopped abruptly and Ogert turned around. He struck Brice across the shoulders with the flat of his sword. A violent anger rose in Darius as she fell to her knees under the blow. Realizing he could do nothing without destroying any chance of rescuing her later, Darius held himself in check. "Ogert is going to pay for that," he muttered as he watched helplessly. The traitor was forcing her to raise her eyes to his face and saying something to her. Just the thought of the sharp edge of the man's sword so close to her throat was making his heart race.

"Is he going to kill her?" Jarn's voice asked.

"No," Darius answered in a rough voice. "If he did, he would have nothing to hurt me with. Ogert knows me too well to do that."

"You know that man?" The surprise in Jarn's voice was unmistakable.

"Yes," Darius admitted. Beyond them, Brice was forced to her feet again. Darius gripped his sword as they moved forward undercover of twilight and shadows. The man was going to wish he had never touched his wife.

They followed until the group disappeared inside the castle. Then all they could do was watch and wait.

"How do you know the man?" Jarn asked softly so his voice could not carry.

"Three years ago there was an attempt on the king's life and he was the assassin that Lord Frehim hired for the job. I prevented him from fulfilling his mission and thus humiliated him. Before he escaped last time, he swore he would have revenge." Darius frowned. "He means to bait me by taking my wife."

Brice lay where she had fallen for a few moments. Her ribs were throbbing and her shoulders ached. Soft sobs came from the crumpled heap, which was all she could see of Lysa in the moonlight.

Something creaked off to the left and out of Brice's sight and a block of light cut across the room. "Who are you?" A shaky voice asked in hushed tones.

With great effort, Brice lifted herself from the floor and looked up. A painfully thin woman stood in the doorway. The room behind her was bright with candlelight and the lamp in her right hand bathed her in light. Her hair hung in limp strands over her shoulders and her clothes were crumpled like she had been living in them several days. Clutched in her left hand was a rumpled handkerchief and her eyes were puffy. She shrunk back pulling the door with her as if it would protect her from Brice's gaze. "Who are you?" She repeated timidly, "What do you want?"

Aware that Lysa had stopped her noise and was paying attention to the new arrival, Brice tried to smile. "My name is Brice." Pushing herself carefully into a sitting position, she said, "As to what I want, I want to get out of here." She looked up just in time see fresh tears welling in the strange woman's eyes. She stepped forward and held out the lamp so it lit more of the room.

"Who is she?" The woman waved toward Lysa.

"Her name is Lysa," Brice answered. Lysa sat up slowly, watching the woman with great interest.

Suddenly she pointed at the stranger and declared, "You are the queen."

The woman visibly tried to straighten her back and appear regal, but she suddenly sank to the floor instead. "I wish I were not," she wailed.

Then it all made sense to Brice. "They have been holding you as a hostage."

The queen nodded, set the lamp on the floor, and blew her nose on the already well-used cloth in her hand. "I have been in these rooms for almost three months now. I am almost ready to try to jump out the window, but I am afraid of what they will do if I can't walk afterwards."

"They have not locked the windows?" Gaining her feet and then almost tumbling back onto the carpet again, Brice finally managed to make it the nearest window. The glass panes gleamed in the lamplight. Fumbling with the latch, Brice pulled at the sash. All the bruised muscles of her back screamed, but she ignored them. The window opened and immediately, Brice stuck her head out and looked down. Her heart sank. The ground, black and hazy in the night, was a very long three stories down, much too far to jump. Stepping back, Brice mentally chided herself for her stupidity. *Of course, how could you forget those three long steep stretches of stairs?*

"Besides I cannot leave." The queen crossed to Brice and Lysa followed. The child leaned against Brice as she had in the hall below. Brice slipped her arm around the girl's thin shoulders and gave them a gentle squeeze. Considering how much she had been through, the little one was holding up well.

"Why can't you?"

"They have my sons in the dungeon and will kill them if I leave." Tears made her eyes glimmer in the lamplight

Somehow, this did not seem true. Why would Ogert take her and Lysa to keep Darius and Ewian at bay and then kill off the hostages that remained to keep the king from attacking? "Have you seen them?"

The Queen nodded and dabbed at her eyes. "When they first took the castle, I was taken into the dungeons and they let me see them. They were in this dark and damp cell together. Maler was wounded and feverish."

"I don't think they will kill them," Brice said. "If they did, they would lose their hold on the king." The Queen sniffled and seemed to consider the possibility.

Drawing herself up so she was sitting straighter, the queen declared, "Then we must escape."

Only a few minutes had passed when out of the corner of his eye, Darius spotted movement in the shrubbery to his left. In hushed tones, he asked, "Jarn, did you see that?"

"Aye," Jarn replied. "It looked like someone else is trying to watch the castle."

"I think he has spotted us." Darius watched as the unknown man made his way from cover to cover toward them.

Resting his hand on the hilt of his sword beneath his cloak, he shifted his weight so he would be able to spring at the man if he proved to be a foe.

A moment later, the man approached them across the last open space. Darius realized that it was Trenar right before the man reached their hiding place. Holding out an arm to signal for Jarn to let him approach, Darius stepped back so he could fit in the shelter of their hiding place.

"I thought it might be you," Trenar whispered the moment he caught his breath. "There are very few men in the Kiylin itself. Most are defending the front gates into the city. The servants' village is almost empty, all except for the few of the families who do not have someone on the household staff. Karyn says someone has had control of the castle grounds for weeks now and everyone she knows has been escorted outside the castle walls. She has been watched so she has not dared to try to alert anyone outside. I told her most of the city already knows."

"Ogert is behind this," Darius interjected. "Do you know if there is anyone else behind it all pulling his strings?"

Trenar's voice reflected a frown. "I wondered why it was so badly organized. No, I have not seen any evidence of anyone else. Is it possible that Ogert is insane enough to leave himself no escape?"

Darius ruefully considered the man that had nearly killed him three years before. "Yes, it is possible."

"I can see he wants to get to the king. Why else would he be holding the queen and all four princes captive in the castle with him? But I had the impression he blamed you, Darius, not the king."

"He does blame me," Darius responded as the pieces began to fit together in his head. "I would wager Lord Micrey was initially pulling his strings, but Micrey did not plan on dying."

"What?" Jarn's tone dripped with disbelief.

"Ogert was initially only following Lord Micrey's plan when he took possession of the castle, but somehow he found out that my wife was on the grounds. He was never one to miss an opportunity."

"You mean Brice is in there with that madman?" Trenar asked.

"Yes." Darius closed his eyes and willed his brain to think. "We arrived right after she and Lysa, Ewian's middle child, were abducted. Jarn and I trailed them here. Was there any way you could have been followed after you entered the city?"

The dark outline of Trenar's head moved from side to side. "I was watching and saw no one."

Jarn turned back from looking around the edge of the low wall that sheltered them. "Another group of men just left the building in the direction of the walls."

"That is odd," Trenar observed. "There were only a few in the entire place when I investigated earlier. What could that man be thinking?"

"I don't know, but I am going to find out." Darius turned to Trenar. "Where is the best way to enter unseen?"

"The kitchen garden," Trenar answered and understanding what Darius had decided, he declared, "I am with you."

Darius simply nodded and turned to Jarn. "Are you coming?"

"I might as well," Jarn answered saucily. "You might need me to save your skin."

Darius grimaced. Thankful that the darkness hid his face from the man's scornful eyes, he turned and checked to be sure the way was clear. Then without waiting to see if the other two were ready, he dashed across the open space in the direction of the kitchen gardens.

Once the decision to try to escape had been made, the Brice started searching for a way to lower them out of the window. A relatively quick search of the sitting room, where she and Lysa had been dumped, yielded no results.

The Queen was reluctant to allow Brice to search the other room beyond, but after a long heated discussion, Brice finally made her understand the necessity. The Queen finally agreed, given that she was allowed to oversee everything Brice touched. Brice was amazed at the woman's inconsistency. One moment she was meekly sniffling into her handkerchief and the next she was a towering royal livid with indignation that Brice had even the audacity to want to search her sanctum.

Just as Brice and the Queen started exploring the bedchamber, the lock on the outside doors began to turn. Lysa who had been lingering in the outer sitting room ran to warn the other two. Brice, who heard the noise, looked up in time to see the frightened child running for the nearest hiding place. The Queen did the same. Brice looked about for a weapon to defend herself. She was not going willingly this time. Spotting a small letter opener laying on the desk against the wall, she reached for it. Right before the men appeared she had it hidden in her skirts.

"Where are the others?" Hameal asked when she turned to face him. Ogert was not with them, but she could see the other two men from before following him into the room. Brice shrugged and looked the traitor straight in the eye. Keeping her face carefully blank she tried to ignore the men as they began searching the room. "Where are the old lady and the child?" Hameal approached her threateningly. His sword was still in its scabbard at his side. Stopping at the point where she had to look up to see him, but too far for her to do any damage without his seeing it coming, he leered at her. "Be a good girl and Ogert might let me have you after we kill Darius." He licked his lips. "I will be kinder than he."

A shriek from the closet announced the discovery of the Queen. Hameal glanced toward the sound and Brice made her move. She aimed for the gap in his leather jerkin near the center of his chest. Either she had made a sound or her movement caught his eye, but the dull knife made it only half the distance before Hameal caught her hand. He did not release it though. Slowly he tightened his grip on her fingers.

"Cry out, girl," he hissed. Brice looked up to find cruel amusement in his eyes. Pressing her lips together, she held her silence defiantly. Hameal tightened his hold again. Brice could feel the bones and joints in her hand straining against the pressure. The rough wooden handle of the opener bit into her palm. Pain shot up her arm, but she had been in pain before.

"We found the old woman," older guard announced. Hameal did not respond and Brice refused to drop her eyes in defeat. This man was not going to have her willing obedience even if it meant him crushing her hand. "What are you doing, Hameal?" The man asked.

"Teaching the wench a lesson," Her opponent grunted.

"Ogert wants her in one piece."

"I don't care what Ogert wants. She tried to stab me and I am going to teach her a lesson." The pain increased as his fist closed more. Brice caught her breath and tears blurred her vision, but she did not make any other sound.

"You don't care that I want her whole?" The question came from the doorway into the sitting area. "Hameal, release her hand." Ogert, looking angry and impatient, glared at his underling. Behind the leader, there stood another man whom Brice had never seen before. He was carrying a brace of lighted candles.

Obediently Hameal released her hand, but as soon as he did, he struck her hard across the face. The strong bitter taste of blood filled her mouth. She was sure that her lip had split. Brice refused to give into her desire to touch it or turn away. Instead, she glared at him.

"You fool," Ogert roared. "Do you want to make Darius so livid he goes battle mad at the sight of her? Can't you manage to leave no visible evidence? I want him rational. He is more vulnerable then." Crossing to her, Ogert knocked the knife from her now throbbing fingers. It dropped with a muffled thud as he shoved a rough piece of cloth into her other hand. "Catch some of that blood before it gets on your dress." Turning the others, he demanded, "Where is the child?"

"Wort is still trying to find her," the man restraining the Queen explained.

"I have her," Wort announced as he emerged from behind the bed and dragged a kicking Lysa behind him by her arms.

"Good." Ogert turned. Nodding to the man who had accompanied him into the room, he said. "Riket, take Darius' wench. Hameal cannot be trusted with her." Seizing the candleholder from the man, Ogert turned and led the way out of the queen's apartments. He informed Hameal of the current situation as they walked down the corridor. "The castle gate has almost fallen and Darius has been spotted on the grounds. I have sent the rest of our men to the gates. I want to choose the battle place before he finds us."

"How is that going to help us?" Hameal asked.

Ogert glanced back at the three captives. Brice met his eyes as she walked defiantly upright. The Queen had returned to her weeping; Brice could hear her occasional sobbing gasps. Although she could not see, the scuffling of the man Ogert had called Wort made it apparent that Lysa had also decided she was not going willingly.

Ogert's cold eyes finally turned back to the passage ahead. "I want to make sure I have every advantage. Come, we do not have much time. I still have to decide whether he or his wench is going to die first."

The kitchen was empty and the hearth bore no sign that a fire had laid there for weeks. Wondering how the invaders were eating, Darius made for the far door. The darkness beyond the opening lay thick and heavy, but he knew his way and did not need the light. The kitchen joined the dining hall via a long corridor with storerooms branching off on both sides. Darius took the stairs at the end two at a time. He could hear the footfalls of his two companions in the hall behind him, but otherwise the place was deserted.

Systematically searching the rooms they passed, the trio made quick progress, but Darius was not satisfied. The sounds of his feet echoed in the great hall as he entered. He glanced around briefly in the unexpected light coming from the windows. The moon must have shone its face. As he was crossing the audience chamber to the throne room, a male yell rent the air closely followed by a child's cry of pain. Looking back to be sure that Trenar had heard it too, Darius tried to locate where the continued whimpering was coming from.

"It's from the throne room." Trenar pointed in the direction of the great double doors to their left.

Darius nodded. "We will enter another way." He turned and headed back the way they had come.

Ogert announced to them all that the place he selected was the throne room. And once they entered, Brice quickly saw why he had chosen it. There were only two entrances and no windows to the large room with lofty ceilings. Holding the candles aloft, Ogert instructed the prisoners to be placed against the wall farthest from both entrances and assigned each of them a keeper.

As soon as she was told to halt, the queen sank to the floor and dissolved into silent tears. She was not going to be much of a challenge for the older man assigned to watch her. Wort dumped Lysa a ways away from the queen so they could not speak without being overheard. Lysa slumped to the floor, brought her knees up to her chin, and glared at her guard over her folded arms. Brice was Riket's charge. He ordered her to kneel to the other side of the queen, closer to the doors and farther from the corner. The distance was such she was not able to offer any comfort to the distressed woman.

Hameal immediately started harassing the child. Brice could not make out the exact words, but she was sure he was being nasty. Then he leaned forward to do something, but he never got a chance. Quick as a flash, Lysa leapt at his hand, the closest part to her, and sank her teeth into the flesh between his thumb and first finger. Hameal roared and backhanded the child to the floor. Lysa screamed in pain.

"Silence." Ogert stalked over, whipping out his sword. Shoving Hameal aside, he pointed it at the child. "Keep your trap shut, brat, or I shall cut your throat. You are only the dessert and I can do without if I must."

Lysa wisely hushed.

"What did you do that for?" Wort asked Hameal.

"The brat bit me." Hameal rubbed his hand sulkily.

"He probably deserved it," Riket muttered so Hameal could not hear. Brice looked up at the man who loomed over her. He was being much gentler than Hameal and the other older man had been. Perhaps he had a wife or daughter like her. He did not return her gaze, but looked steadily forward. A muscle in his cheekbone twitched and the hand resting on his sword was gripping it so the knuckle turned white.

Turning to Hameal, who was still nursing his hand, Ogert shoved one of the candles toward him. "Make yourself useful and light the lanterns that will burn," he ordered.

Hameal moved off in the direction of the nearest lantern, one of many that hung at intervals along the throne room's walls. Even the queen was silent as Hameal slowly lit the room. The illumination grew in patchy glows. Brice guessed some of the lamps were out of oil because Hameal would try getting the flame to catch and then after a time he would move on to the next. Nevertheless, the fine paneling and elaborate tapestries lining the walls progressively came into focus.

The tapestries reminded her of the one she had hidden behind the day that Lord Micrey's castle fell, the day she first encountered Darius. Almost as if her very thoughts summoned him, Darius appeared in the shadows along the opposite wall where three of the lanterns in a row were not burning. It was if he had appeared out of nothingness. Glancing cautiously toward Ogert, Brice realized no one else had seen him. Carefully tilting her head, she looked again quickly. Yes, it was definitely him standing there, silent and almost invisible. Fear rose in her throat. *He came alone.*

Hameal returned to their group. Handing the candle to Ogert, he asked, "How long do we wait?"

"Until he comes." The leader cast a cold glance in Brice's direction. Brice dropped her eyes. She was afraid he would be able to read them.

"He is here." Darius' voice carried well in the vaulted hall. Everyone, but Brice and Ogert, jumped.

Ogert did not even wait to see where Darius stood; he strode over and yanked Brice to her feet. Twisting her arm behind her, he drew his blade, and brought it to her throat. Pain shot up her arm into her shoulder causing her vision to spot. The sharp edge of the blade bit into her skin slightly as Ogert brought her around and used her as a living shield. Brice gave up trying to see at that point. Closing her eyes, she concentrated on not swallowing.

"I have been waiting a long time for this, bastard." Ogert spat over her shoulder. Unclean smells flooded her senses and suddenly, she was struggling not to wretch.

"To kill an innocent girl?" Darius' voice was steady and perfectly pitched, no trace of accent or emotion.

"No." Ogert laughed and the blade edge jumped painfully. Instinctively, she sucked in air and tried to move her throat farther from the blade. "She is only here tonight because of you. You were the one foolish enough to marry her." The smell of decaying food filled Brice's nostrils. The man's grip on her arm tightened as he pulled it higher. Her joints cried out in protest. They had not been made to move in that direction. Brice began to pray she would not pass out from the pain.

"Once you claimed her as yours," Ogert spat, "you sealed her death warrant. Now watch her die." Abruptly he threw her to the floor. Landing on the hard tile on her arm, Brice felt something give, but it was a small detail that was registered in the back of her mind. The rest was occupied with the deadly blade coming down upon her.

Darius did not bother with countering the assassin's blade with his own. He had carefully calculated what the man would possibly do once Darius had announced his presence. Since every possibility centered on Brice, Darius made sure he was close enough to stop just such a maneuver. Once the man's attention shifted from himself to Brice, Darius drew his dagger with his left hand. It only took two quick steps. He linked the man's sword arm with his good right arm thus stopping its descent and jabbed upward with his left, sinking the blade to the hilt.

It took only a moment for the body to go limp, but Darius felt like it took forever. The wound in his upper arm opened again and he could feel the blood soaking his tunic. It was only a matter of time before it would be soaking his cloak as well. In the hushed silence, the queen's scream ripped at Darius' ears. He looked up and managed to bring his sword up just in time to counter another man's attack. Without thinking, he blocked and lunged, dimly aware of the fact that others were similarly engaged.

Somewhere behind him he heard the death rattle of another man. As he turned, he realized that the man who had been guarding Brice was now standing over the dead third guard blood coating his sword.

With great effort, Darius focused on his adversary. *Hameal.* His surprise almost cost him dearly. He dropped his guard for a moment and Hameal jumped at the chance. At the last moment, Darius knocked the man's lunge to the side and made one of his own. It was weak. Hameal blocked it easily.

The pieces began to fall into place. Hameal was the informant who told Ogert about Brice. He also knew where Ewian lived and probably saw Trenar when he was escorting Brice. He was the missing link.

Anger rose and with it his adrenalin. The small burst was all he needed to unarm the man. The sword fell with a clatter a very small distance from Hameal. Darius began to realize how weak he was when he could not hold his blade steady enough to point the tip at the man. The former cook leered at Darius. Looking significantly at the quivering blade, he started to stoop toward his weapon while watching Darius.

Out of the corner of his eye, Darius saw someone move to put their hand on the Hameal's blade and pull it out of Hameal's reach.

"I have him," a voice informed Darius. Ewian's blade came between Darius' and Hameal. "March, traitor," Ewian barked at the cook. "Pray that I am feeling merciful, for I doubt my king would mind if I added one more corpse to the burial heap tonight." Hameal obeyed. Darius rested his blade tip on the ground and closed his eyes.

"Careful, you are swaying." Trenar's voice came through the haze of pain. A hand supported his back and Darius fought to open his eyes. "You don't want to fall on Brice."

Brice? Where is Brice? Darius opened his eyes and turned his head to focus on Trenar. "Where is Brice?"

"Here." A voice came from the floor. "I would stand up, but I cannot even manage to sit." She lay awkwardly on her left arm. Lying at her side was Hameal's blade. Pain darkened her eyes and he could see new bruises darkening parts of her face and neck. Dried blood crusted her lip. Her dark hair was messed and hung in limp strands. She was the most beautiful sight he had ever seen. Smiling weakly, she said, "I think it is broken."

"Where is Kurt when we need him?" Darius asked and smiled in return. Carefully sheathing his sword, he gingerly touched his own upper arm.

Trenar grimaced at the blood soaked material. "You both need a healer. I will see what I can do." He made his way across the hall toward the doors of the main entrance.

"I guess they managed to get through the gates," Darius said trying to distract himself from the pain. He felt so weary. *I am getting too old for this.* It was not the first time that the thought had crossed his mind. *But this time I have something to strengthen it.* He looked down at Brice. Now was not the time for them to talk, but they were going to have to do it soon.

Part VI

"What a lovely couple you make," Kurt exclaimed sarcastically fifty minutes later in the servant's room he was using to examine patients. "At least she follows directions," he informed Darius as he started cutting away his tunic sleeve. "You on the other hand…" The healer frowned at the torn flesh before replacing the blood soaked pad. He started shuffling through his bag one-handedly while continuing to apply pressure to the wound.

"How bad is she?" Darius asked just as the healer pulled out his scissors and packet of needles.

"She will be fine. Time will heal the bruises and the arm." Kurt switched hands and started sterilizing his instruments in the lantern he had lit earlier for the purpose. "She was more worried about you than herself. Your slow responses and unsteadiness on your feet were her two main concerns. Don't worry; I assured her that it was most likely from loss of blood." Darius turned his head away as the healer took up the scissors. Minutes later the old stitches removed and the new covered with a snug bandage, Darius rested his head against the wall behind him.

"Kurt, have you ever heard of a mercenary learning a trade?"

The old man's hands stilled. "What are you thinking?"

"I am not indestructible and I am getting older."
Darius sighed. "I cannot go on forever and for the first time, I
find myself wondering what will happen tomorrow." He slit
his eyes open and watched the old man's face. It was still.
Opening his eyes all the way, he asked, "Have you ever heard
of a man of my profession doing something else?"

"I have." The healer did not look up as he resumed
clearing up. Finally, he turned to Darius. "Lean forward," he
commanded. Darius obeyed. Taking a band of strong cloth
cut for the purpose, he looped it under the left forearm and tied
it behind Darius' neck. "Don't use the arm at all, and this time
I mean it, and take this every morning and evening with your
meals. You know the dosage." He placed a small packet of
powder into Darius' good hand. With that, the healer left, and
Darius leaned his head back again and closed his eyes.

Brice was waiting outside the door for Kurt to finish.
The healer looked tired and grim. "Darius?" she asked.

Kurt looked up and an amused smile touched his
mouth, but his eyes were worried. "He will be fine. In a
month, it will be just another scar to add to his collection and
bother him in his old age."

"May I see him?"

"He is just inside," Kurt answered. "So do you two
have somewhere to go tonight? His quarters have not been
occupied in months."

Brice smiled reassuringly. "Karyn told me that she
will have it ready when we get there."

Kurt nodded and turned to go. Brice had placed her
hand on the door handle, when he called her attention back to
him. "Brice." He waited for her to turn. "He is coming
around. Give him time."

Brice opened her mouth to ask what he meant, but he
did not wait. *Coming around to what?* Shaking her head at
the man's curious behavior, she opened the door and slipped
inside.

The healer had left the lantern lit. A soft glow from the flame made only half the room visible. A single bed and chest were against the left wall and Darius sat on the only chair against the right wall. He did not move at her entrance, so Brice silently closed the door and leaned against it.

He was pale beneath the olive tones of his skin. Deep circles ringed his eyes and his scars stood out darkly. Beneath his eyelids, his eyes roamed; he must have fallen into sleep during the brief period since Kurt's departure. Brice was hesitant to wake him, but he needed real restful sleep. He was not going to get that sitting upright in a chair.

"Darius," she whispered. His eyelids stilled and his breathing changed. She spoke again, this time slightly louder, "Darius." His eyes opened and gradually focused. Painstakingly, he turned his head and fastened his gray gaze on her.

"Hello, little bird," he murmured. A shadow of his usual smile pulled at his lips.

"Karyn and Timothy are preparing your house for us." Brice stepped away from the door toward him. "We should really be heading in that direction."

"Not until I speak with the King." He leaned forward and slowly rose. Staggering slightly, as if not sure the ground would stay beneath his feet, he one-handedly straightened his tunic. Brice crossed to gather his cloak from the bed where it had been tossed. The dark stain made her pause. The material would always carry its mark. Still, he needed the warmth for the trek home. She lifted it and turned to help him put it on. Meekly, he allowed her to fasten it around his neck and lay it carefully over his shoulders. Then turning, he led the way out into the hall.

The castle corridors were no longer empty. Armed men moved this way and that, some sporting scrapes and bound wounds from their long battle for the city. Scattered among them were servants just returning. No one noticed the unusual pair as they passed among the lot; at least not until they were crossing one of the great halls outside the throne room.

"Darius." Trenar's voice echoed through the room and a majority of the occupants turned to watch Trenar approach them. "I have been looking all over for you." He glanced at Brice's sling and nodded. "So, you have seen a healer then. Good." He took Darius by his right arm. "Come, the king wants to see you." He guided Darius toward the throne room door. Brice followed reluctantly. *He needs to be in bed.*

Inside, the King was waiting with a group of men she did not recognize. Someone had brought in a table and placed it in the center of the room. They had also filled the empty lamps, for now the room was luminous and she could see clearly the blood stained floor and scattered weapons left from skirmish.

Trenar led Darius straight to the king and Darius managed a shaky bow. Brice hung back, forgotten. "Ah, Darius." King Jenran acknowledged him. "I have heard everyone's account of what you have done for me this day. My queen and sons have been rescued from the hand of a madman and my castle delivered into my possession with barely any bloodshed."

Darius started to protest, but the king raised his hand to silence him. "I am aware that you are not the only one to do this. Trenar and Jarn will also be rewarded, but you are the one that has faithfully served me. You are the one who has now saved the life of each person in the royal family. This is a debt I cannot ignore." Taking a piece of parchment from the table, he began to read.

"In recognition of the outstanding valor and loyalty of our personal guard, Darius Aarin Laris, we do decree that he is released from our service. From henceforth we bestow upon him the title of Lord Wyner and all the lands and privileges therewith, including a permanent place on the advising council to the King. He will have the right to bestow by marriage the title of Lady to the woman he chooses to wed. The title shall pass on to his heirs in whatever manner he deems best. The throne of Braulyn will not interfere with his choice. This decree is binding and legal to the full extent of the law, etc, etc."

The king raised his eyebrows and regarded Darius over the edge of the parchment. "Do you accept the commission, Darius?"

"If my wife wishes," was the answer.

Brice thought her heart would stop as a murmur passed through the group of nobles gathered around the table. Darius turned and the king stepped forward so he could meet her eyes.

"What do you say, Brice?" King Jenran asked. All eyes turned to her. Brice swallowed and concentrated on Darius' face. *What does he think he is doing?* His eyes were clear despite the pain pulling at his features. His face impassively gave her no clue as to what was going on behind it. A new title and her old master's lands were being offered to him and he was laying them in her hands. Suddenly it dawned on her. He was giving her a choice. He trusted her to make the right decision for both of them. Even though she knew the answer, Brice did not answer. Instead, she stepped forward so she was at his side. Taking his hand in hers, she looked up at him expectantly.

"We say yes, my king," Darius said. "I accept the commission, granted I can now go home and sleep. My wife is weary and so am I."

Jenran laughed, "Yes, Darius, go home. We will work out the details tomorrow."

Darius bowed, Brice curtseyed, and they left.

The cool predawn air greeted them as they stepped beyond the doorsill. Brice filled her lungs in one deep breath. Darkness still cloaked the sky, but the horizon beyond the city to the east glowed with the promise of morning. Above her head, the inky blackness was speckled with points of light and a light breeze brushed her cheek.

Darius stood farther down the path. He had continued when she paused. Turned back toward her, he extended his hand in much the way he had the night they had been married. "Are you coming?" he asked.

Unlike their wedding night, Brice looked and found no fear in her heart. Without hesitating, she stepped forward to place her hand in his. Just as it had before, his large warm hand gently enclosed hers. She watched the movement of his fingers for a moment before looking up to meet his dark watchful gaze. "Thank you," she whispered. "Thank you for the choice."

He smiled; her heart answered. "Thank you for your answer." He dropped his eyes. "Are you ready to go home?" Accent tinged his voice.

She nodded and then stepped closer. Standing on tiptoe and pulling him down by his good arm, she brushed her lips against his cheek. "Yes."

Darius turned his head and before she could back away; he kissed her. She must have released his hand for it was suddenly in her hair. His fingers cradled the nape of her neck and his thumb stroked her cheek. Her world centered on this man standing over her; focused on his lips, his touch...him.

The following week was a whirlwind of activity. Darius had no time to recuperate. There were papers to sign and regulations to learn. He previously had some understanding about the duties of a titled landowner, but he never imagined the magnitude of paperwork he processed in those first two days. The only time he was not reading or signing was the time he spent with his eyes closed for sleeping. He saw Brice moments before his head hit the pillow at night and as he gulped down his breakfast in the morning.

On the third day, the steward that he hired to keep things organized informed him that he needed to take possession of his lands in person as soon as possible. By noon, Darius' few essential possessions had been added to the heap of supplies in the new wagon he was surprised to find he owned. The street before Darius' house filled with well wishers and the men-at-arms that the king had insisted Darius take to smooth the claiming of his new lands. Timothy and Brice appeared right before they set out. Karyn gave Brice a quick hug and presented her with a small bundle. Darius was not able to catch what she said, but Brice smiled before obeying Timothy's beckoning and moving toward the waiting caravan. Shortly after settling Brice on the wagon, Timothy mounted and they were off.

They made slow progress through the city, but once they cleared the gates they picked up the pace considerably. The roads between the capital and Lord Micrey's old stronghold were dry and in good condition. The steward declared it should only take them a few days to reach their destination. Darius did not care about how long as much as the fact that he still had not gotten a chance to speak with Brice. Glancing frequently over at the supply wagon and Brice perched next to the driver, he considered exactly what he wanted to say.

He still was not certain what exactly had inspired him to choose her that last day of the siege, but he wanted her to know that he was thankful he had. He missed her company those few days they were parted. There was a deep desire in his heart to get to know her better. She was complex and intriguing. In fact, he looked forward to spending the rest of his life doing that.

As much as he was burdened with wanting to tell her, he knew that he was not likely to get a chance. Traveling in a group and at the fastest speed possible meant they were not going to stop until the last possible hour. Then all the time would be consumed with setting up camp and preparing the meal. Falling into bed and instantly asleep would only be followed by an early rising to begin again. There was going to be no time for the long conversation he desired. Looking yet again at the figure on the carts, he decided to wait until there was more time.

They arrived at their destination in the mid afternoon of the seventh day. The moment the wagon and company halted in the courtyard, mayhem ensued. Their procession through the village attracted a crowd of curious followers and the steward lost no time in putting anyone he could manage to work. Brice watched the dashing to and fro from her perch on the wagon seat. She looked across the heads in search of Darius. She spotted him about to enter the main doors, deep in conversation with the captain of their armed escort.

Timothy was directing the unloading the wagon. Deciding she could be of some use in that area, Brice carefully climbed down from the seat. Going around to the back, she scanned the bundles for one that looked like she could manage one-handed. Her broken arm no longer pained her all the time, but Kurt had been very clear in his instructions not to use it yet. Spotting one that looked small enough, she reach across the gate for it only to have someone else grab it first.

"Oh no, you don't," Timothy declared. "If Darius caught you, he would have my head."

"Then what else can I do?" she asked.

"Go see the steward." Timothy nodded in the direction of the main doors. "I saw him go in there."

Brice worked her way across the yard, dodging carriers and soldiers. When the heavy oak doors smoothly closed behind her, Brice heaved a soft sigh into the welcome emptiness of the entrance hall. It was much dimmer than the bustling space outside. High above, slits in the thick walls allowed a mean measure of afternoon sun to enter. Debris and over turned furniture littered the floor. Picking a way carefully around the tapestry that had once hung opposite the entrance, Brice headed for the opening on the left. Darius would have most likely wanted to see her master's former chambers. If the estates old records had escaped the looters, he would have a much easier time assessing his new property.

The halls were dark and she heard voices dimly from other parts of the castle. She saw no life in this wing until she reached her old master's quarters. Lord Micrey had enjoyed all the luxury his income and lands could provide. As a child, Brice had been inside his private rooms. Entering the sitting room area, Brice could see very little changed since that one time so long ago. The steward's voice came from the direction of the bedroom instructing someone on what had to be done before the new lord retired for the night. He continued speaking as Brice tried to determine what to do. Darius was not here.

Suddenly the man burst back into the room and came to an abrupt halt. "My Lady." He regarded her with raised eyebrows. A frown flickered across his features so briefly Brice was not certain she had not imagined it. Bowing stiffly, he said, "Your quarters are in the opposite wing, my lady. Do you need a guide?"

Brice suppressed the frown she felt and pulled every up last ounce of dignity she had left. "I know the way, thank you, steward. I was looking for my husband."

The man stared into space for a moment and then said, "He did not say where he was going." Then he pointedly turned his back and left the room.

Brice had a sudden urge to scream, but she figured it would only make things worse. Turning on her heel, she stepped back into the corridor. Figuring she could continue to look for her elusive husband on her way to her new suite, she made her way the opposite direction. She was taking the long route.

An hour later, she found herself outside the familiar doors of her mistress' rooms. She had seen almost every member of their party except her husband and her feet hurt. Tentatively she pushed the door, which opened with a low groan. In the light from the lamp she acquired in her wanderings, the splintered wood of the doorframe littered the stone floor.

Evening was turning into night and if she wanted to make sure she had a bed she had better investigate her new home. Stepping carefully, she moved further into the room and lifted the lamp. The shadows receded and revealed the remains of chairs and an overturned table. Shredded tapestries littered the floor and her former mistress' personal belongings were thrown about. Sighing, Brice reminded herself that she had been looking for something to do. Setting the lamp on the floor, she started with righting the table.

Darius rested his forehead against the wall of his new hall. The cold stone felt good against his skin. His head was throbbing and all he could think of was of finding Brice and a soft place to sleep. *Now where had that man said my quarters were?* Pushing off from the wall, he took the lantern off the table and headed in the direction his foggy brain told him was correct.

He had not seen his steward since they arrived and the slacker sent Darius to evaluate the defenses. Darius finished that task hours ago. Since then he had been going from one job to the next and people kept popping up asking him favors. They always premised the request with "Your steward said." Here it was about midnight and his steward had not even shown his face. Wasn't he supposed to be helping Darius with his duties, not disappearing and sending more work Darius' way? Deliberately pulling his mind away from the subject, Darius pushed open the door that supposedly led to his rooms and entered.

Candlelight illumined a large high-ceilinged room. The great fireplace that dominated the far wall glowed and a meal was spread out on the table before it. A large chair stood waiting for him to sit and eat, but Darius was more eager to see his wife. It would be their first time alone in a week and there was much he wanted to tell her. "Brice," he called as he walked to the open door leading to the bedroom.

"She is not here, sir." Timothy appeared in the opening with a concerned look on his face. "I had hoped she had found you."

"What do you mean?" Darius frowned. *If that steward had anything to do with this, he is going to be thrown out instantly.* "I have not seen her."

Timothy frowned also. "The steward said something about her looking for you and then grumbled something about a lady's place is in her quarters."

Darius gritted his teeth. "Where are the mistress of the house's rooms?" he demanded.

"I believe they are in the far wing. I thought it odd the two were so far removed."

"It was common knowledge that Micrey did not like his wife, Timothy. I thought you knew that."

"Yes, but I would not have guessed..."

Darius did not let him finish. "Find that steward and bring him here." Then turning, he strode toward the door.

"Where are you going?" Timothy asked.

"To get my wife." Darius slammed the door behind him and stormed back toward the other wing. He did not even pause to wonder how he would find the correct suite until he realized he was walking in darkness. *It is too late to go back now.* He decided and pressed on.

It took only moments for him to reach the other side of the fortress. None of the rooms he passed were occupied. Doors hung off their hinges and reminders of the attack only a few months before were everywhere. Darius was just beginning to wonder if he should have hesitated long enough to find a guide when a meager glow appeared under a door farther down the hall. He quickened his step.

Brice shivered and pulled her traveling cloak closer around her shoulders. Leaning over the grate of the fireplace, she adjusted the chair legs so they lay closer to the sputtering flame she coaxed into life by burning a piece of the ruined tapestry. Then she watched anxiously for the fiery tongues to lick at the raw wood where it had splintered. It caught tentatively.

Satisfied that it would burn if she gave it time, she leaned back on her heels and carefully rose. Her back and her arm hurt, but the floor was clear. She had found a broom and swept. Now it was a clean barren space, and she was going to tackle the task of making herself a bed. The feather mattress on her mistress' bed was slashed beyond repair. The thought of the gutted thing sent shivers down her back. Darius had saved her from more than she had realized.

Turning, she walked slowly into the other room and began looking for the maid's cot. She found it behind the wardrobe and was in the process of trying to pull it out when she heard the groan of the outer door. Letting go of the cot, she immediately went to investigate.

"What are you doing here?" Darius demanded the moment she appeared.

Caught between the overwhelming delight of finally finding him and concern because he was obviously irate, Brice found she could barely manage to speak. "Trying to make a bed," she finally managed. "I found the old maid's cot behind the wardrobe in the bedroom and was trying to pull it out."

Darius grimaced. "Leave it there. You won't need it. Come." Holding out his hand, palm up, he waited for her hand. "I went to my new rooms expecting to find my wife waiting, and found she was not there. I don't know why you are here, but you are coming with me."

"I thought you wanted me here." Brice did not take his hand. Instead, she watched his face. "Your steward said I was to come here. I looked for you, but no one would tell me where you were, so, I assumed you wanted me here."

Darius dropped his outstretched hand with a sigh. His face did not relax, but he was no longer grimacing. "Brice, you are my wife." His voice was deep and thick with accent. "That makes you more valuable to me than any position, property, or servant. I can always get another steward—in fact, I have already set my mind on it—and I can live happily without lands and title." He pinned her with his eyes, "You, on the other hand are not replaceable and I want no other wife." He paused and watched her for a moment. "I don't know how to say it more clearly," he said softly and dropped his eyes.

"I love you, too," Brice whispered.

His head snapped up at the words and then slowly he smiled. Brice could not help smiling in return. Darius did not wait this time, but crossed the space in a few strides and enclosed her within his arms.

His embrace was painfully tight and Brice was almost smothered in the folds of his tunic, but she found she did not want him to stop. Finally, after a moment, he stepped back. "Come, I am hungry and I am sure you have not found much to eat in this mess. I left a wonderfully smelling meal and a soft bed to find you. Will you come share my meal and my bed?"

"Aye, my lord," Brice answered and Darius laughed.

The End

Author

Rachel Rossano loves hearing from her readers. If you would like to write to her and tell her what you thought of *The Mercenary's Marriage*, her email is Anavrea@yahoo.com. She also maintains a blog and websites: www.xanga.com/anavrea, www.freewebs.com/anavrea, and www.geocities.com/crownofanavrea.

Other Books by Rachel Rossano

The Crown of Anavrea

Printed in the United States
204665BV00001B/49-57/A

9 781420 925128